THE
NORTHERN
ELEMENTS

THE NORTHERN ELEMENTS

A Novel

'The North remembers.'
Game of Thrones

Quirinal Press
LN2 5RT

Cover image (copyright pending) with thanks to
Blackburn with Darwen Library & Information Service:
www.cottontown.org

IN FOND AND GRATEFUL MEMORY OF

St John's C of E Junior School
Blackburn

BY THE SAME AUTHOR

Martin, a Novel

Humphrey and Jack, a Novel

A Dish of Apricots, A Novel

Cherries

The Mouse Triptych

The Swan Diptych

Come Away, O Human Child

PART ONE

Shades of the prison-house begin to close
Upon the growing boy

William Wordsworth
Intimations of Immortality

ABOVE ME WERE CONCENTRIC RINGS OF BRICKWORK, funnelling out of the gloom to the top of the chimney. The light up there seemed no bigger than a shilling, though dazzlingly bright. The squarish rungs continued on upwards but those nearest the top were lost in the light haze, so I could not count how many more there were still to go. Looking down I could see an elliptical patch of dim light on the ground, thrown from the open boiler door.

'Where are you?' another boy's voice shouted. It sounded a very long way away.

'About halfway up,' I shouted back.

'You're a bloody liar, Tommy Catlow,' said the other boy.

'And you're an effing coward, Peter Shawcross,' I shouted. 'You wouldn't even get in the boiler.'

'Chicken!' Peter yelled.

'Wet wazzock!' I cried.

Clucking hen noises floated faintly up to me.

They were right. I was terrified.

Looking down was dizzying and I tried to avoid it. Looking directly up was impossible because of the blinding brightness of the circle of light at the apex of the chimney. There was nothing for it but to keep on climbing. The rungs had been spaced at a distance from each other which would be convenient for an adult but rather testing for me. I would not be eleven until October - three months away.

We had heard about the disused factory in Little Harwood from some older boys at school. They said it was easy to get into and that it was really spooky.

The Northern Elements

So one summer Saturday, we decided to miss out the matinee at the pictures and go out there and explore. There were Peter and me, Dennis Flitch, Mike 'Turdy' Brown, and little Willie Melling, who looked like an albino.

Perhaps he *was* an albino. I don't know.

Peter was nominally the leader of the Brookhouse gang but I was the 'ideas' man and I received plenty of respect for that. There was always a measure of rivalry between us, even though Peter was my best mate.

We met by the lamp post outside my house on Brookhouse Lane at half past ten. Little Harwood was a suburb to the northeast of the town, about a mile away. I had suggested that we badger our mums for butties and pop because we would more than likely be out all day. This usually worked because our mothers would be only too glad to get us out from under their feet. Willie had forgotten his lunch, but after a quick consultation with Peter, it was decided that we had enough between us to feed him. Besides, Mum had given me some money for toffees so nobody would starve. We were eager to be on our way - it was better this way than sending him home to get supplies. He lived on Enamel Street - or Animal Street, as we called it - and we couldn't risk him getting lost. He was only eight, bless him.

I had dithered about whether to take my dog, Mick, but thought that we might be climbing fences so I decided to leave him at home. This had made Mum suspicious.

'What are you up to, young man?' she said. 'Why can't you take him? He'll be following me about and moithering me all day.'

'I dunno, Mum,' I said. 'Peter just said we had to travel light.'

'And what does that mean when it's at home? You weren't going to carry the blasted dog, were you?'

'I'll take him for an extra long walk tonight. I promise I will. On me mother's grave.'

'Never mind my grave, you cheeky bugger. If that boy told you to put your head in the fire, would you?'

'Nah, course I wouldn't. Do you think I'm as daft as you, Mum?'

And I fled before she could catch me, banging the door after me. Behind it I could hear Mick set up a pitiful howling.

At last we were off, down the lane to the Bottom where the Blakewater ran, sometimes lurid with dye, and up the other side towards St Urban's, the alien Catholic church. On Larkhill, we stopped at Mrs Wilkinson's dark little shop, where she made her own sarsaparilla and sold it in bottles, without any label, for a penny a shout. We shared two bottles between the five of us and then turned down Cobwall to the Plane Tree pub and up the hill to the war memorial clock tower.

So far we were on familiar ground because the Star cinema was just by the clock and we would usually come here on Saturday mornings for the ninepenny matinee.

But today we were spurred on by a more challenging enterprise. Up Whalley Old Road we went, turning left into Providence Street, just where the hill becomes much steeper. There was a strange smell in the air: thick, rich and sweet, but too powerful to be pleasant. Turdy said it was malt being toasted in the nearby Lion Brewery where his dad worked. He knew this because his dad had once taken him on a tour.

The older boys had been accurate with their directions. At the end of the quiet cobbled street there was indeed a derelict factory. At first we were daunted by the fence. This was made of thick wire netting, stretched between concrete posts. These posts were angled inward at the top and barbed wire extended along the entire length of the fence except for the gates. Following instructions we made our way along to these. They were made of chipboard attached to metal frames. The wood had been kicked and then prised away until there was a gap, allowing access for the bigger boys with a bit of a wriggle. For us, there was no problem.

We were awestruck by the sight which lay before us. There was a huge empty yard. Grasses and thistles had already thrust their way up between paving stones, some of which were cracked. There was an air of desolation and the place was totally silent. Even the pigeons and sparrows seemed to have deserted it. It was as if we had stepped into a different world. There were various out-houses including a warehouse with a loading bay, which had a raised brick platform, above which a jib crane jutted from the wall. Every window had been broken and splinters of glass which stuck out from the frames, glinted in the sunshine and emphasised the blackness within.

Bigger than all the other buildings put together was the workshop itself. We approached the metal doors with their sooty high windows with something approaching reverence. Older and stronger boys had done our work for us. They had rocked on the door on one side and half-wrenched it from its hinges. As before, it was easy for us relative squibs to squeeze through.

Here was the biggest empty indoor space I had ever seen. It was vast. The floor was covered in thick dust, though it did not obscure the rectangular greasy lines which showed where machines had once stood. I had no idea what had been manufactured here so whether the lines marked the shapes of lathes or looms I couldn't tell. Here and there, haphazardly, machine parts lay on the floor. Against one wall, broken wooden pallets had been roughly stacked.

There were footprints in the dust but not many. They looked like those sheets you lay on the floor in order to learn dance sets. They were doubtless the prints of the older boys who seemed to have become bored very quickly. Or perhaps some other part of the site had interested them more.

High above us was a saw-toothed roof where ridges ran the length of the factory and panes of glass were set at an acute angle to each other. These were mostly intact though they had been covered with mosses and algae. Through this came a green submarine light which filled the space. The dust on the factory floor became the sea bed upon which dwelt the metal skeletons of long-dead aquatic creatures. We moved forward in the underwater silence, stopping occasionally to examine machine parts and then laying them down again, none the wiser.

At the far end of the expanse, we passed through open doors into the boiler room. At least, that is what we assumed it to be. There was a big fat metal tube affair which took up most of the room. At the end nearest to us was a circular door which could be opened and shut with what looked like a car's steering wheel, but made out of metal and massive. I think we fully expected it not to work but Peter gave it a turn and it opened easily enough. Then when he turned the wheel and closed it again, there was a satisfying clank as the mechanism locked the door.

'Right, who's going in?' Peter said.

Everybody was curious but nobody was particularly keen, so little Willie Melling was 'volunteered'. It didn't take much to persuade him. He was so chuffed to be allowed to join our gang and share in our adventures, tiny as he was, that he could usually be persuaded to do anything for the price of a sherbet dip. He could be pushed to the top of a high wall with railings above it, for instance. Once up there, he would tie a rope to a spike and the rest of us could climb up. Once, when Dennis had locked himself out of his house, we pushed Willie through a tiny kitchen window. He was like a loyal fox terrier. We could have used him for rabbiting.

'It's dark,' Willie said, looking in and hesitating. 'I think there's a bit of light at the far end though.'

'I've got a torch,' said Dennis. He was always the practical one amongst us.

Armed with the torch and the promise of liquorice shoelaces as well as a sherbet dip, Willie climbed through the boiler door. We clustered around it and watched the wandering torch beam as Willie gave us a commentary.

'It's big, but there's nothing in here. Wait a minute.'

The torch beam went out and then came on again.

'There's light coming through a little arch on the floor. Hang on - it's a tunnel made out of brick. It's not very long. I'm going in.'

'He thinks he's in a gangster film,' said Peter.

There was a silence and just a pinpoint of light at the end of the boiler. Then we heard Willie shout:

'Bloody hell fire!'

Willie had recently begun to experiment with swearing in order to impress us. The effect was more comical than awe-inspiring.

Soon we saw the torch beam swinging about. Willie was back in the boiler and coming towards us. We helped him clamber out through the door.

'Bloody hell fire!' He said again. 'It's bloody fantastic.'

'What is?' we clamoured.

'You go to the end of the boiler, right? And you go through this brick tunnel, right?' This was his moment of glory and Willie was milking it for all it was worth. 'And you are *at the bottom of the chimney!* Bloody amazing! You can see the sky at the top. It's just a little circle. It must be miles high.'

'Well, more like 300 foot or thereabouts, I reckon,' said Peter. What do you think, Turdy?'

'About that, yeah, probably,' Turdy said.

'Yeah, but listen...' Willie was not finished yet. 'There are rungs in the wall that go all the way up to the top. You could climb up.'

'Why didn't you, Willie?' Peter said and everybody laughed - except Willie who looked crestfallen.

'Because my legs are too short!' he said and everybody laughed again. Willie cut the laughter short by saying: 'But *you* could, any of *you* could.'

'Could any of *us* get through the tunnel?' Turdy asked. He was the biggest and could perhaps see where things were going. Maybe he was hoping Willie would say: 'Not you Turdy - you're too big.'

But Willie just said: 'Any of you. Easily.'

'Right,' said Peter, 'who's it going to be then?'

'You're the leader - it should be you,' I said.

'But what if I had an accident? You'd be leaderless.'

'We'd manage,' I said.

Peter ignored me.

'Turdy?' He said.

'It should be somebody light,' Turdy replied, looking at the dusty floor.

'Dennis?'

'Nah! Asthma. You know I've got asthma,' Dennis said. He took out his inhaler and used it ostentatiously.

'That leaves...' said Peter, slowly and ominously.

'Tommy!' cried the others in unison.

'Bastards!' I said.

'You're best at gym,' Peter said. 'Anyway, *I dare you.*'

This was getting very serious. Our honour code was binding.

'*I double dog dare you!*' I replied. This challenge was not to be used lightly. If you failed in such a challenge you could be thrown out of the gang. You would be an outcast for the rest of your life.

'All right, you asked for it. *I triple dog dare you!*'

There was a profound silence.

I had been trumped. There was no escape. This was utterly sacred and there was no higher challenge. It could only be issued at moments of the gravest importance and if you refused it, you had to commit suicide like the Romans.

That is how I found myself inside the chimney and nearing the top. Sweat was running down my sides and into my eyes, making them smart, and my arms and legs were aching. There was a sharp metallic pain in my upper arms and thighs. But the light was getting brighter on the walls. Just before the top, the rungs turned into a real ladder and at last I emerged into the daylight.

1890   BREAD

FIVE BOYS MET UNDER THE GAS LAMP at the corner of River Street and Higher Audley Street at ten o'clock, as arranged. It had been raining for days but that was nothing new in Blackburn. The damp air was good for the cotton, they said, and anyway, the boys had never known anything different.

They all wore cloth caps and mufflers. Two of them wore clogs and three were barefoot despite the cold and wet. You got used to it. There was Daniel Catlow, the leader of the gang; Richard Clayton, the brightest; Robert Harrington, the biggest, and James Bibby, the practical one. Little George Pickford was late.

'He'll mar everything if he doesn't show up soon,' Danny said.

'Let's go without him,' said Richard. 'Wherever it is we're going. What's it all about, Danny?'

'You'll see,' Danny said. 'It's James's idea really. But we have to wait for Georgie. We need him.'

After a minute or two, Robert shouted: 'Here he is!' - and sure enough, George came hurtling round the corner of Withers Street, passing through the patches of pale light which hung in a damp aura around each gas lamp and through which thin rain continued to fall. In the darkness between two gas lamps, he slipped and fell in a puddle but soon recovered.

'I'm sorry, Danny,' he blurted out when he reached them. 'I accidentally let the sneck of the door go with a clack and I thought me dad were moving about, but it's all right now.'

'Are you sure?' Danny said.

'Aye, he'll have got up for a pee and gone back to bed. He's not bothered about me any road. He couldn't care less.'

Though none of them was older than ten, they had had little trouble getting out at this hour of the night. All of their parents worked at River Street Mill, apart from Richard's dad, who was a clerk at the Gas Board. The others used to try teasing him about it, claiming that it made him 'posh', but he wouldn't rise to it. All of their parents were dirt poor, worked extremely hard, and went to bed early, exhausted. In any case, they couldn't afford to spend money on candles and lamp oil after eight o'clock at night. The knocker-up would be rattling on their windows with his long pole at five the next morning. They needed all the sleep they could get. Besides, sleep was a blessed relief from labour.

The exception was Danny's father. Danny had lost his mother in an accident at the mill two years ago and since then his dad had been on the sauce. He'd be in The Wellington or the Cicely Hole Hotel until chucking out time, which would be soon.

'Now then lads, we need to get our skates on,' Danny said, 'We don't want to bump into my dad. He's been dead mardy lately.'

'Right,' said Richard. 'Georgie's here now. What's going on?'

'You hungry?' Danny asked.

'Course we're hungry. We're always bloody hungry,' Richard snapped. It was no fun standing about in the rain. 'What are you on about?'

Richard was getting frustrated with Danny's air of mystery. Though the two of them were close pals, there was sometimes friction between them.

'All right, don't get your knickers in a twist,' said Danny. 'What we're going to do is this. We're going to do Hargreave's Bakery on Eanam. You're going to go to bed with full bellies tonight lads, and there'll be some left over. Come on, let's get a move on. We'll get down to the tram shelter at Foundry Hill and I'll tell you the plan.'

They set off, close together, half-walking, half-running until they reached the railway bridge on Cicely Lane where, rain or no rain, they stopped to look down the line at Blackburn Railway Station. Rob Harrington had to lift Georgie up so that he could see.

There was a passenger train in the station where the engine was taking on water. From here on the bridge, they could hear a kind of panting and then, from time to time, a thud and a great hissing exhalation of steam, rising up the sides of the engine and closing over the top. In the dark, they could see the faint and fuzzy points of the gas lamps on the platforms, seeming to converge only to disappear in the rainy murk. Much brighter was the red glow from the firebox of the engine, leaking out on either side of the black monster.

'That is so beautiful,' said James Bibby dreamily. He was obsessed with trains.

'Where's it going?' asked George.

'That one will be going to Glasgow,' James said, 'via Hellifield and Carlisle.'

'Where's Glasgow?' George said.

'It's in Scotland,' said James. 'That's another country, Georgie.'

'How will it get across the sea?' George asked.

'Magic,' said James.

Just then, steam issued from behind the wheels, smoke billowed from the funnel, and the train began to chug towards them. In a few moments, they were enveloped in smoke that smelled like coal. They rushed to the other side of the bridge and the white smoke began to stream over their heads. They could see the rain as if it were suspended in the smoke. The passenger coaches passed beneath them, throwing light from their windows onto the stones of the cutting on either side. Sparks flashed on the gravel and there was a squealing noise. At last, only the red lamp at the back of the guard's van was visible, rapidly dwindling to a point. A melancholy whistle announced that the train was taking the bend at Daisyfield and the excitement was over. There was only the cold and the rain.

The last tram was leaving for Accrington when they got down to Eanam and they took refuge in the wooden shelter while Danny explained the plan. It was good to get out of the rain.

'You see Hargreaves' shop over there next to the Bowling Green pub?' said Danny.

They all knew it well and nodded.

'We're not going to break in are we?' said Richard, 'I'm not so keen on that.'

'That's the beauty of it,' Danny said. 'We don't have to. There's a back lane behind for deliveries to the pub and for the bins and the like, right? It's easy to climb into Hargreaves's yard. Me and James climbed in the other night, didn't we?'

'It were a walkover,' said James. 'There's a window in the yard to the bakery at the back of the shop. Now this window has got louvred glass in it, see?'

'What's loofahed?' George asked.

'It's strips of glass set into the frame at an angle,' James said. 'It's probably to let the steam out when he's baking or stop it getting too hot, or summat.'

'Oh, I get you now,' said George as if he'd known all along.

'Thing is,' said James, 'you can take the glass slats out so one of us can get in.'

'And we can put them back afterwards,' said Danny triumphantly. 'and nobody'll know how we got in!'

'What if Hargreaves hears us?' said Richard.

'Don't be daft, Rich,' said Danny. 'He's always up at three o'clock in the morning doing his baking. He'll be out like a light at this hour.'

'What about the girl?' Richard said.

'What girl?'

'Her as works in the shop.'

'She don't get in till near seven o'clock. She don't live in.'

'How do we know there's anything worth nicking?' said Richard. He didn't want to sabotage the plan but he was getting a bit jealous of the attention James was getting and the fact that they'd done a recce without him. He was supposed to be Danny's lieutenant after all.

'We thought of that,' Danny said. 'James has been keeping a watch. Tell 'em, James.'

'Right, I skived off school for the day. Did Concrete Head say owt when he took the register?'

The other boys shook their heads.

'Tosspot, he is. Anyway, I watched Hargreaves' shop all day,' James continued. 'Now then, Tuesdays are not good for business round here. Wednesday's payday for the mills, and the foundry and Thwaites' Brewery - that's tomorrow like. So old Hargreaves won't have done a lot of trade today. He'll be putting today's bread out tomorrow and saying it's fresh. He's tight as a duck's arse, he is.'

'Meantime,' Danny took up the story, 'he'll keep today's bread out the back. Tomorrow, he'll mix it up with a fresh batch and it'll all go. He'll be stampeded tomorrow dinner when every bugger has their pay.'

A lonely hansom cab clip-clopped by. There was no other traffic at this time of night. The rain had stopped and a full moon peeked tentatively from the receding clouds.

'Are we up for it boys?'

The five boys put their fists together.

'Champion,' said Danny. 'Now this is what happens. We get over the wall. Me and Danny remove just enough glass for Georgie to get in.'

'Why me?' said George.

'Because you're the smallest,' James said.

'Do I not get a say?'

'No,' said Richard. 'Shut your gob.'

'Now, if the coast is clear and there's owt worth nicking, we pull Georgie out and one of us goes in and passes the swag out.'

'I'll do it,' Richard said. He was eager to claim back his proper status from James.

'Good lad!' said Danny. 'Let's go!'

They ran across the street, crouching like soldiers under fire, as seen in *The Boy's Own Paper* that they could read in the Library. They ran through the ginnel between The Bowling Green and the bakery. There was muffled shouting and singing from the pub. They must be having some kind of shindig in there. All to the good. It would give the boys a bit of cover.

Robert, who was the biggest, gave them a leg up and, one by one, they went over the wall. It had been agreed that Robert should remain as lookout and would give the gang whistle in the unlikely event that anyone should come along.

Gingerly, Danny and James began removing the glass. James took off his haversack and produced a length of rope which they tied under George's armpits. They had no idea how long the drop was beyond the window and didn't want to take any risks.

'It's dark in there,' George whispered. 'How will I see?'

'Sssh!' said James. 'I've thought of that. He produced a lantern he'd made out of a tin can with holes punched in. It contained slow-burning cotton waste soaked in the oil from tinned sardines. A wick was coiled in the bottom and protruded from the top. The contraption was suspended from a cradle of string and James had even brought on old mitten so that George wouldn't burn his hand.

Danny and Richard lifted him through the window and James lit the makeshift lantern with a single match. It smelled vile but produced a serviceable light.

'I don't need the rope,' George whispered and he passed it back. 'I'm standing on a shelf and I can get to the floor no problem. Give me the light.'

James passed it to him and they could see it moving about the bakery like the will o' the wisps they'd seen up on Darwen Moors.

Suddenly, the sash window upstairs went up with a roar and a man stood there with a candle.

The boys froze.

'Who's there?' Hargreaves said. 'Who's in my yard?'

1960   AIR

AT THE TOP OF THE LADDER WAS A METAL HANDRAIL that curved over at the summit of the chimney. I grabbed it with both hands and climbed onto a kind of viewing platform. In front of me was the lip of the chimney, a brick wall that came up to my breast. Behind me a rail ran around the inner circumference. There was a gap in it from which a lightning rod emerged. The rail gave me the courage to move around the platform. It had been hot and still down below. Up here there was an appreciable breeze, though not strong enough to cause alarm. In fact, I felt safer up here than I had on the rungs.

The view was breathtaking. Lancashire lay all around me like a many-coloured map. My geography of the county was pretty good. I owned an Ordnance Survey map of Blackburn and Burnley [Sheet 95] and Peter and I used it to cycle all over the place.

I emerged facing south-west. Before me lay the town. I could make out King George's Hall, the Town Hall and the Market Hall clock tower. There was the cathedral and the train station and the bus station on the Boulevard. The green buses looked like Dinky toys. Bolton Road snaked southward and I could see the Royal Infirmary and the green rectangle of Ewood Park where the Rovers played. Up on the moors, Darwen Tower stood like a stumpy black rocket. The whole landscape bristled with church steeples and factory chimneys.

To the west was the triangle of Corporation Park with its lake and conservatory and, at the top of the battery, there were two concrete cradles for cannon captured at the battle of Sebastopol during the Crimean War - the cannon themselves had been melted down in World War II. Beyond lay Preston and the flatlands of the Fylde. I wondered if the shining white line on the horizon might be the Ribble Estuary and the Irish Sea beyond.

To the north were Pye's Wood, Cunliffe Quarry and Little Pudding, a tumulus shaped hillock, all favourite playgrounds of ours. Beyond, here and there, were thin strips of bright silver ribbon which must surely be the River Ribble. The grey-blue ridge in the hinterland was Longridge Fell.

Eastwards, I could see the cooling towers at Whitebirk shaped like the diabolo set I had been given at Christmas. Even from up here they looked like great white giants exhaling clouds of steam, rising in slow-moving puffs to dissolve into the flawless sky. Beside them, the gleaming line of the Leeds and Liverpool canal struck north-east towards the gloomy shape of Pendle Hill, where witches and bogarts dwelt. On the horizon ran the blue Pennines, which we believed God had created to separate us from the barbarous people of the White Rose, who worshipped strange gods.

Everywhere there was purple moorland, dotted here and there with reservoirs like gleaming coins. It was so exhilarating up here that I quite forgot the agonies of the climb. If only I had a camera!

I remembered the triple-dog dare. If I had a camera I could prove that I'd made it to the top. How else could I do that? Peter would not just take my word for it and the others would follow his lead.

Then I had a brainwave. I fished my hanky from the pocket of my shorts. In the corner, sewn in blue silk, was the initial 'T' for Tommy. I had been given a packet of three handkerchiefs for Christmas, crisp with starch and pristine white. This one was crisp with dried snot now, but so what? If I threw this over the lip of the chimney and into the yard, it would prove that I had climbed to the top.

But just a minute. What if the breeze wafted the handker-chief out of true and it floated onto the factory roof, or it just got lost altogether? It would need to be weighted somehow. Up here, there was plenty of birdshit and even the bedraggled re-mains of a nest but no sign of a stone or a pebble that could be used to ensure a straight drop. I felt in my pockets again. I couldn't risk my latchkey and besides it was not that heavy. My fingertips lighted on my beloved pen knife. I pulled it out. It had a green tortoiseshell handle and it had been my companion for as long as I could remember. I couldn't even remember how I'd acquired it.

I was deeply unhappy about risking it out of my sight, let alone throwing it down the chimney, but I thought of the sacred dare, and the risk of losing it seemed better than being obliged to fall on it. I placed it in my hanky and tied it into a secure parcel. The edge of the chimney top was too broad for me to lean over and just drop it. Sending up a prayer for the preservation of my penknife, I hurled it out into the air and it plummeted out of sight. I have to admit that anxiety for the knife was mixed with elation. If it landed safely in the yard and could be retrieved, it would be proof positive that I had completed the quest and that would be one in the kisser for Master Peter Shawcross.

But first, the descent. This was even more hair-raising than climbing up. Gripping the rails, I went down the ladder, but that was the easy bit. The rails continued alongside the first four rungs. If they had not, I would never have made the transition and would have clung there, at the bottom of the ladder, until doomsday. I couldn't look up because of the dazzle and I daren't look down. Facing the dirty bricks and groping with my feet, ever so slowly, I climbed down the chimney.

When I reached the bottom, my legs were like jelly and I was quivering all over. I rested for a few minutes to get my breath back and got down on all fours to crawl through the tunnel. It was only when I emerged into the boiler that I realised there was only a faint ambient light filtering in from the chimney and nothing from the door. I moved to where I thought the door must be and banged on it and shouted. Nothing. My so-called friends had shut me in.

31

1890   PIES

HARGREAVES LEANED OUT OF THE WINDOW, peering into the yard which was washed with pale moonlight. The boys stood stock still against the wall below him, hardly daring to breathe.

'Who's that in my yard?' Hargreaves said again.

Richard could see George's light moving about inside the bakery and prayed that he wouldn't take it upon himself to come to the gap in the glass and make his report now. Even whispering would be fatal.

'Bloody cats!' Hargreaves said and slammed the window down.

'What's going on?' said George appearing at the bakery window. 'Shush,' said Danny. 'It were Hargreaves upstairs but he's gone back to bed now. Quiet as a mouse all the same. What've you found?'

'I don't need this now,' George whispered, handing over the makeshift lamp. 'I can see by moonlight. Is Rich coming?'

'Is there any bread?'

'Loads - and barm cakes and oven bottoms - and pies!'

'Right. I'm going in,' said Richard.

'Here,' said James and he produced a pillow case from his haversack. 'You can put the stuff in here. I nicked it from Old Ma Higson's washing line yesterday.'

Richard climbed into the bakery and disappeared into the gloom. Danny and James waited for what seemed an age, their eyes fixed apprehensively on Hargreaves' window. At length, they saw Richard's face in the bakery window, white in the moonlight.

'Are you there?' he whispered.

'Yeah,' Danny replied.

'Right, here comes George,' and he lifted the little lad out to the others, followed by the bulging pillowcase. The yeasty smell was glorious. Last of all, Richard clambered out himself.

'There's three potato pies in there,' he whispered triumphantly.

'Champion,' said Danny. 'Get 'em over the wall to Rob. Take Georgie. Me and James will put the glass back.'

Richard lifted Georgie onto the wall and passed the bag up to him and he passed it down to Robert. Then George jumped into Rob's waiting arms and Richard climbed over. The other two boys were not long in joining them.

'Job's a good'un, lads!' said Danny. 'Come on!'

They ran soundlessly to the ginnel and across to the tram shelter where Danny reached into the pillow case and produced the first of the pies, tearing it into portions. Even cold, the spicy meat and potato filling and soft, moist pastry were bliss. The three pies were gone in no time. They made short work of a couple of two pound loaves, ripping off chunks and cramming them into their mouths.

When their bellies were taut as drums and they couldn't eat another crumb, there were still plenty of barm cakes and another loaf left in the pillow case.

'I'll get up early and go round th'houses - see if I can't flog them,' said Richard, who was keen to get back in Danny's favour. He watched James but there was no reaction. 'There'll be plenty as is broke before they get paid at dinner time. I might get a few pennies - no questions asked.'

'Shall us see if they want us to take dinner orders at the mill?' said Danny as they walked back up Cicely Lane.

This was a good sign, Richard thought. Danny was conspiring with him again and not James.

Taking dinner orders meant going into the River Street Mill around eleven o'clock, by which time the workers would have been paid and would have drawn up a list of who wanted what from the bakers. The boys would take the list down to the shop and bring the hot pies back. The mill hands were happy about that because it meant they wouldn't have to waste any of their precious dinner hour queuing in the bakers.

The lads would have to put up with people saying: 'Shouldn't you be at school?' but they were used to that and nobody cared much anyway.

'I want to see if we can tell owt from Hargreaves's face,' Richard said.

'Nah, he's allus a bad-tempered bugger,' said Danny. 'I'd rather get a chance to see his face first thing in the morning when he sees half his stock gone and he can't work out why.'

'It'll send him doolally,' Richard said and they burst out laughing.

'Ey, Rob,' Danny turned to where the others were walking a few paces behind, 'Rich and me are going to skive off after play-time tomorrow morning. Tell Concrete Head that Rich sprained his ankle playing British Bulldogs and I had to take him home.'

'Give over. He'll never believe that,' Robert said. 'You'll get the ruler.'

Their class teacher was pretty handy with the ruler across the palm of the hand. Once, James was called to the front of the class for talking out of turn.

'Six!' Mr Bamford shouted. 'Hold out your hand.'

James did so but jerked it away at the last minute.

'Do that again and I'll double it!' said Bamford.

James did it again.

'Twelve!' Bamford shouted.

James did it again. By the time he got to forty-eight, Bamford was purple with rage and the class hysterical with laughter.

'You little devil!' Bamford had shouted, grabbing James by the wrist and holding his hand steady. He only administered six but the strokes were vicious. James had walked back to his seat with tears in his eyes but a big grin on his face.

Later, he showed his classmates that Concrete Head had actually drawn blood. This made him a hero, especially with the girls.

Richard knew that the others would be thinking of that occasion as they reached the point where the gang would be splitting up.

'If James can take it, we can,' he said. 'Can't we, Danny?'

'Aye,' Danny replied. 'It'll be worth it.'

'What are you doing?' said Georgie. 'Can I come?'

'No,' said Danny.

The next morning, Richard did not get a chance to speak to Danny till playtime. He was dying to tell him that his door-to-door bread sale had raised twopence three-farthings. Everybody could see that Danny had a black eye but Concrete Head had said nothing so they would have to wait.

After an endless lesson on multiplying fractions, they were allowed out into the playground. It was not raining but the sky was sullen and grey. Everyone crowded around Danny.

'What happened?' they clamoured.

'Mind your own bloody business!' Danny roared at them and they dispersed, muttering.

Richard and Danny used the waste bins at the back of the school to clamber over the wall and into the back alley.

'What did happen?' Richard asked.

'Me dad was still up when I got back. He were that drunk he were skenning like a basket of whelks. I said he were a drunken pig and he punched me in the face. I went round to me Auntie Elsie's and she let me stay even though it were late.'

His dead mother's older sister lived on Maudsley Street, just round the corner. Danny had often gone round there for shelter when his dad was on the rampage. She was a formidable woman and his dad would never face up to her - not that he would be capable of it considering the state he was in. Besides, he had loved his wife and respected his sister-in-law.

Within minutes, the boys were in the weaving shed at River Street Mill. The door had been open to let some air in. It might have been dull but it was a hot August day all the same. Inside, the noise was colossal.

They were stopped at the entrance by the foreman, Dick Ramsbottom, who was a sarcastic bloke with a face like a billy-goat. Nobody liked him.

'Where do you think you're going?' he shouted above the din.

'To see me Auntie Elsie for the dinner list,' Danny shouted back. 'We'll not be long.'

'Aye, well mind you're not,' the foreman said.

'Right you are, Mr Ram's-Arse,' Danny said when they were out of hearing and he waved two fingers at the man's departing back.

They found Auntie Elsie at her loom.

'Have you got the dinner list?' Danny mouthed.

The Northern Elements

Northern women had developed, over time, a special way of exaggerating the movement of their mouths so that their friends could lip-read what they were saying over the racket of the looms. It was called 'mee-mawing'. Kids quickly picked it up. It was handy in the classroom if you were up to mischief.

So now, Danny stuck his tongue out on the 'th' of 'the' and held the tip of his tongue on the 'l' of 'list' a little longer than usual.

Auntie Elsie nodded. She continued to work the loom but looked down towards the bulging pocket of her pinafore and nodded to Danny to fish out the contents. Here was the list, scribbled in pencil on a torn scrap of paper, and money wrapped in a hanky.

'Get yourselves a potato pie between you. And there's thruppence for you, an' all. Jug's on the bench,' she mimed and her mouth opened wide on the word 'pie'. The bench she mentioned ran the length of the shed and, sure enough, near her loom was a basket with a tea towel in it to keep the pies warm. The jug was for gravy. Hargreaves would fill it and cover it with a little cap of greaseproof paper, twisted at the corners. They would have to try to get it back to the women without spilling it.

The boys had no difficulty understanding her. That was what they were there for. There would have been a little collection of farthings for their tip. Women smiled and nodded at them as they made their way out.

38

On the way, they came across a couple of men sitting on the steps of another part of the factory. Whilst the boys were inside the sun had come out. The men had found some excuse to share a fag in the sunshine. They were more intimidating than the women.

'Dodging school, are you?' one of them said. 'I'll tell the master over you.'

'Leave them alone,' the other said, laughing. 'Can't blame them on a nice day like this. Any road, there weren't no school for us when we were childer.'

'Where's your dad today, Danny Catlow?' the first man said. 'He didn't clock in this morning.'

'Dunno,' Danny lied.

'He'll be out on his arse, if he carries on like this, you know,' the first man said. 'You tell him.'

Danny just nodded. Where would he be if that happened, he thought. Auntie Elsie had her own family to bring up. And anyway, he loved his dad. He wouldn't be like this if his mum hadn't been and gone and died on them.

But the dark thoughts only lingered a moment, chased away by the sun and the prospect of a potato pie, hot this time.

Richard told Danny about the two pence three farthings he had raised with his bread sale. Together with the three pence they were earning now, that was a farthing short of a tanner.

They were rich.

1960 PROOF

I DON'T KNOW HOW LONG I KNELT THERE at the door to the boiler. Long enough to realise that the fear I experienced whilst climbing the chimney was just a faint tremor compared with the black horror that flooded me now. Long enough to be absolutely certain that I would die in the dark and that my white bones might not be discovered for centuries.

It was probably about three minutes.

I heard a grating sound and the door opened. For a second I was dazzled by the green light but then I leapt at Peter and knocked him to the ground, my hands on his throat.

'You bloody swine, Shawcross,' I cried. I was sitting astride him. He was stronger than me but I thought I could manage one good punch to his face before he threw me aside. I pulled my right arm back but it was too late. The others pulled me off him and away, holding me back, while I spluttered and cursed.

Peter propelled himself backwards on his bottom for a few paces before standing up and dusting himself down. He probably knew that he would have won in a straight fight but I had clearly unnerved him. He kept his distance though he was safe enough. Turdy had my elbows in his grip and even little Willie was standing in front of me, his hands flat on my chest.

'Come here, you bastard coward!' I shouted, rather pointlessly under the circumstances.

'Calm down,' Peter said. 'It was just a joke!'

'Some bloody joke!' I cried, wriggling to get free. 'I thought I was going to die in there.'

'Oh, grow up,' he scoffed. 'We wouldn't have left you.'

'I didn't know that, did I? You complete tit!'

'Yeah, well...'

'Yeah well, what?'

'Yeah well,' Peter had recovered himself by now and was turning sly. 'Maybe you would have deserved it.'

'What do you mean - "deserved it"? How could I have deserved it?'

I stopped struggling. Turdy's grip was beginning to hurt.

'Come on,' I said. 'How could I have deserved it?'

'The triple dog dare,' Peter said. 'You said you would climb to the top - and you didn't.'

'I did. Who says I didn't?'

'I do,' Peter said. 'Dennis and me went into the yard and watched. No way did you get up there.'

'It's true,' Dennis said ruefully. 'We didn't see you.'

'That's because the rim was too broad,' I said. 'You wouldn't see me from below.'

'Oh yeah? Your mother might believe you - thousands wouldn't,' Peter said.

'Tell him to let me go,' I said. 'and I'll prove it to you. I promise I won't belt you.'

'Yeah, right, you and whose army?'

I was quiet by now.

'Just tell him to let me go.'

Turdy let go of my elbows and Willie scuttled away. I stood rubbing my arms.

'Right, where's this proof then?' Peter said.

'I threw summat off the top,' I said.

'What?'

'You'll see.'

And I walked past Peter and across the vast factory floor and its aquatic light, out into the sunshine of the yard, the gang following behind.

We walked around the perimeter of the main shop floor until we reached the base of the chimney. There was the outside of the brick tunnel through which I had crawled. For a few long moments, hope left me. I scanned the ground meticulously but there was nothing but gravel, fag ends and an empty crisp packet.

'What are we looking for?' Peter said in a sarcastic voice.

I ignored him.

Suddenly, I saw a gleam where I hadn't expected it. I had thrown my little parcel out into the air as hard as I could and had been scouring the ground at a little distance from the foot of the chimney. However, gravity had exacted its force in a true perpendicular and the gleam proved to be the metal of my penknife right at the chimney base. The impact had broken it. The green tortoiseshell casing had come away on one side. A little further off, the handkerchief lay still in the hot breathless air. I picked everything up and held the evidence out, the broken penknife in my left hand, and the snot-starched hanky in my right, making sure that they could all see the 'T' for Tommy sewn into the corner.

'You can see that this is mine,' I said, waving the hanky. I turned to Peter and held out the broken penknife. 'And you know this is mine,' I said. 'You've borrowed it often enough. How could it have got here if I hadn't thrown it from the top? Tell me that, eh?'

'You could have dropped it on the way in,' Peter said desperately.

'But we didn't come this way,' said Turdy.

'Yeah, don't be a cloth head,' Dennis said, 'we didn't even know there was a way inside the chimney when we first came in. It's obvious Tommy cracked it.'

'Tommy did the triple dog dare! Tommy did the triple dog dare!' Willie chanted, capering around in a circle as he had probably seen Red Indians dancing in some western.

Peter looked at the ground for a while and then looked up, smiling.

'Well done, our kid,' he said. And he came over and shook my hand.

At that moment, invisibly and wordlessly, the leadership of the gang passed from Peter Shawcross to me. Nobody ever said anything, but it was a fact.

43

I stood there, looking down at my broken penknife. The casing was not broken but it had come away.

'I can fix that for you, if you want,' Peter said.

'We'll never find the screws,' I said. 'They're tiny.'

'My dad'll have some,' Peter said. I handed over the knife. I realised that this was a gesture of homage on his part and I was gracious.

'What are we going to do now?' said Willie.

'We've come this far out. We might as well go blackberrying!' I declared.

And that is what we did: my word was law now. Up Whalley Old Road we trooped, across the arterial road, beyond Sunny Bower and into the countryside. We scoffed our butties - mine were salmon paste; I don't know about the others - and drank our pop, sitting on a stile. Then we set about the brambles in the hedgerows along the road, which were abundant with fruit all the way to the New Inn. There were other kids there but there was enough for all.

Exhausted, our arms scratched to ribbons, our fingers stained purple with the sticky juice, we tramped happily home, bearing leaking carrier bags bulging with blackberries. Mum sent me to the Co-op at the corner of Brookhouse and Whalley Range for a couple of Bramley apples and, by the end of the afternoon, the sweet scent of blackberry and apple pie filled the house.

1890   WATER

IT DOES NOT ALWAYS RAIN IN LANCASHIRE. True, the saucer of hills, in which Blackburn lies, seems to invite more than its fair share of damp and drizzle. Even when Atlantic storms have raged over Ireland and spent the last of their fury over the Irish Sea, there is enough of the wet stuff to mizzle over the fells and to lacquer the melancholy pavements and cobbles of the town. For the poor, winters are long and harsh.

But the sun shines on rich and poor alike and, even if he shines hotter and more often on 'that London' than he does on the lads and lasses of the North, who is to doubt that the northerners relish exposure to the sunshine all the more?

It was the weekend after the burglary and Daniel and Richard, James and Robert were in a state of high excitement, and little George was beside himself. They were going swimming.

When the weather was good, they often did this. Usually, they would walk up through Corporation Park, past the fountains, past the statue of Flora with a basket of stone flowers on her head, around the lake with its ducks and swans. They would cheek the old men on the bowling green:

'Go on, you old git, you couldn't hit it if it were as big as King George's Hall!' Danny would shout.

Richard would join in: 'Watch yourself bending over, Granddad! You might never get up again.'

'Less of your lip, you saucy buggers!' they would reply. 'Show some respect for your elders and betters. Go on, get out of it.' And the boys would scarper, perhaps to the playground with its climbing frame and monkey bars. They would stand on the swings to get more leverage with their knees until they were swinging above the horizontal. They would get Robert to push the roundabout while the others sat on it urging him to run faster and when it was spinning dizzily and Georgie squealing with delight, Robert would leap on board himself. Or they would stand on the higher bars of the steel umbrella, rocking it as it turned so that it clanged dangerously against the supporting post. Or perhaps they would climb Devil's Rock, or the even steeper Angel's Rock, up to the Barbican and sit astride the cannons which had been captured in the Crimean War.

Only when the sun was high, and their shirts sticking to their bodies, did they make their way down to Four Lane Ends and on to Tom Crook's Delph. This was really a disused quarry that had flooded. Parents and grandparents warned them away from it with dire tales of death and misadventure. Men whose businesses or marriages had failed had drowned themselves there, they said. Farmers had drowned puppies and girls had drowned unwanted babies. And boys, just like them, had been caught by the ankles and dragged underwater by forces that no-one could explain.

It was true that a strange silence hung over the surface of the water which mirrored the sky. It was said that the Delph had no bottom. They supposed this couldn't be literally true but Dan and Robert, who both liked to dive and to swim underwater, said that they couldn't reach it so it must be very deep indeed. None of the tales of death and despair deterred the boys in the least and the haunting quiet of the place would be shattered by their shouts and laughter as they splashed each other and ducked and dived. Grazing cows looked up in surprise and then resumed their munching. Little George, who could not swim, would busy himself happily, building a little cairn with stones at the water's edge.

But today's plan was much more ambitious than this. They were going to swim in the Ribble. Unlike the dirty Blakewater, the Ribble was a proper river, with bends and rocks and deep pools and rapids, and the tug of moving water against your body was more exciting than the cold stillness of the Delph.

Their destination was the ferry point at Dinkley, near the Roman village at Ribchester. They pooled their money. There was the threepence that Richard and Danny had earned from taking the pie order; there was tuppence three farthings Richard had earned from selling the stolen bread; James had another tuppence stolen from his mother's purse, Robert, practical as ever, had one and tuppence ha'penny that he had been somehow saving for a second-hand bike, and even little George Pickford had a silver threepenny bit he had saved from his Christmas pudding. Nobody was bothered about the illicit provenance of James's contribution or the disproportionate size of Robert's. They had two shillings and a penny farthing - a royal sum. They could afford to buy some pop and to catch the tram to Wilpshire. From there it was a three-mile walk to the river.

They caught the tram on the Boulevard early on a Saturday morning in late summer. It was grand to climb the spiral steel stairway and to sit on the open top deck as the tram rattled and clanged and squealed its way out to the suburbs. They were told off by the conductor more than once for clambering over the wooden seats and they would settle until he went downstairs again, when they would resume their game. At each stop they heard him shouting: 'Plenty of room up top!' But they had the upper deck to themselves for the greater part of the journey.

Soon, the rows of terraced houses began to give way to brick-built, semi-detached mansions with stone porches, rhodo-dendrons and gravelled drives and then, beyond Brownhill, there were fewer houses altogether, apart from many-windowed mansions behind high walls, belonging to mill owners and other magnates.

From their vantage point at the top of the tram, the boys had glimpses through the trees of green velvet lawns, tennis courts, and stone terraces with stone balustrades. Once, they caught sight briefly of a woman with a lilac dress with a bustle, a matching parasol over her shoulder. With her were two girls with frilly white aprons over their lemon-coloured dresses. The boys said nothing but were conscious of another world, like an illustration in a book, visible but unreal.

There were trees arching over the road now and flashes of sunlight. Robert stood on one of the benches, reaching up to pull leaves off the branches just above his head.

'Give over, you dozy get,' Richard said. 'You'll topple off the side of the tram - and I'll tell you summat - we won't be coming back for you.'

Meekly, Robert sat down again.

Soon they arrived at Wilpshire's quaint little station, a rural halt with its tubs of geraniums, so different from the smoky black din of Blackburn's busy station. A long goods train was passing through and James would not move until the last wagon had passed beneath them.

'Where's it going?' asked George.

'China,' said James as the group moved on.

'What's it carrying?' George continued.

'Treacle,' said James, 'from the treacle mines at Tockholes.'

'Get out of it,' said George laughing. 'You don't get treacle from a mine.'

'All right, Smartypants, where do you get treacle from?' said James.

'From a *tin!*' shouted George triumphantly.

'Aye, but where does it come from *afore* it goes in the tin?' said James.

'I dunno,' said George. 'Where does it come from, James?'

'From the mines,' said James, 'like I told you. And the mines at Tockholes are the deepest in the world so the treacle is the blackest. That's why it's so prized in China - they put it in their tea.'

George turned to Robert and said: 'Is he pulling my leg, Rob?'

'Only about the China bit,' Robert said.

'So where is that treacle train really going?'

'Yorkshire,' said Robert. 'They haven't got any of their own.'

'Can you not stop him blathering?' said Danny, who was walking ahead with Richard. 'He's like a blooming parrot.'

'Leave him alone,' said Robert.

James had caught up with the leaders, leaving George and Robert to follow them a few yards behind. They made a comical pair: Robert was well over five foot tall while George still some way short of four. He scuttled alongside Rob, looking up at him, and bombarding him with questions.

Their route took them along footpaths and bridleways and across fields down into the deeply wooded valley of the Ribble where the stream was wide, yet still relatively young and fast running. The hay had been cut some weeks before but in the bright sunshine there was dust in the air. On the other hand, there were still signs of recent heavy rain on the paths. In places, the hedgerows had grown across the footway and they had to struggle to get through. In other places stinging nettles were high and dense. Here and there were puddles of standing water where cattle had sheltered under trees and their hoof prints had filled with water which reflected the blue of the sky. Near the stiles, were fresh cow pats, with gold-coloured flies crawling on the surface.

Nevertheless, to these town boys, this was Paradise. George frustrated the older boys because he had to keep stopping to examine things and ask Robert questions. He found a multi-faceted piece of quartz and wanted to know if it was a diamond. What were those purple flowers, he asked. Rob, who could identify a dandelion and a daisy, and perhaps a rose, if pushed, had no idea. When a group of cows came up a sloping field towards them, Rob was a little uneasy. However, they were just curious and when the bell cow lowered her great head to inspect George more closely, he was in raptures.

'Why do the flies crawl about round its eyes like that?' he asked.

Again, Rob didn't know. He just said: 'Because flies are bastards. Come on.'

Danny was getting a little frustrated at the slow progress they were making. He knew the way because he had been taken down to Dinkley when his mother was alive. He couldn't let George and Rob fall too far behind, but the sun was high, the day was hot, the boys were sun-dazzled and sticky with perspiration, and they couldn't wait to get into the cold running water of the river. Eventually, Rob hoisted George onto his shoulders and they caught up with the others at the turnpike road which Danny said went all the way to York. The boys made the ceremonial spitting noise, customary with them whenever Yorkshire was mentioned, and crossed the road, taking the footpath opposite. It took them gently downwards until, after several more fields, they saw suddenly, through gaps in the trees, the sparkling river.

They had been walking for an hour and a half but now they broke into a run and tore off their clothes on the southern bank, stepping cautiously across a shoal of sand and water-smoothed rocks, arms outstretched for balance, to throw themselves naked into a kind of pool on the other side of a bend.

1960   ALONG THE RIVER

AT SCHOOL, THE DAY AFTER THE BLACKBERRYING, Peter showed his loyalty by presenting me with my penknife, fully restored. The tiny screws in the casing looked a little too new and shiny but they would soon wear. To reward him I told him to meet me after tea by the lamp post. I said we would be having an adventure without the others, just me and him. He begged me to tell him what it was but I told him to wait and see.

Tea was pea soup made with a hambone, with chips floating in it. I loved it - and so did Mick, the dog. Whether on purpose or not, Mum would always drop three or four chips on the kitchen floor as she was serving them up and Mick would dive on them and toss them up in the air to cool them before snaffling them. I wolfed mine down in double quick time and asked permission to leave the table. I changed from my school shoes into pumps and said I was going out.

'Where are you going?' Mum asked.

'Ah, that's for me to know and you to find out,' I said and pulled my tongue out at her.

'You'll come to a bad end, you will, you cheeky bugger,' she said, and added: 'Take the dog.'

I mused for a moment. It would be tricky but we'd manage.

'*Jawohl, mein Führer,*' I said, giving her a Nazi salute and went to get Mick's lead from the cupboard under the stairs. He knew what was happening and went berserk, doing a couple of circuits of the living room, barking madly, before he came to submit to having the lead attached to his collar. He was only a mongrel but he was devoted to me and I loved him even though he was daft as a brush.

Once outside, I let him off the lead and stuffed it into my pocket. Mick would stick with us, or, if he ran off, he would always come back. There was much less traffic about in those days and besides, he was quite a canny dog.

Peter was at the lamp post and we gave each other the special gang handshake which involved a complicated interlocking of fingers. Then we went to Ben's.

Old Ben lived in a house a the bottom of Brookhouse Lane just before it turns up towards Larkhill. We knocked on the door and he let us in. It was always gloomy inside because Ben kept the curtains pulled tight in all weathers, even during the day. He was probably not as old as we thought he was but, because he was completely bald and had lost an eye in the war, we thought he was ancient. He wore a black eyepatch like a pirate which, I suppose, was part of his fascination for us. He always wore a striped shirt without a collar, a shiny black waistcoat and a thick belt with a huge buckle.

One of the reasons I went to visit Ben, usually on my own, was because of his books. He was an obsessive collector and had a room full of them upstairs. He would sit reading at a battered bureau in the corner whilst I sat at a table in the middle of the room leafing through illustrated encyclopaedias or one of Ben's books on the occult. I learnt that I was a Scorpio, that I was passionate, loyal to friends and a born leader, but that if you crossed me I would be a ruthless enemy. My planet was Mars and my symbol was ♏ - this seemed to fit perfectly and I drew an ♏ on all my school exercise books for luck.

But books were not the reason we were here today. Right in the middle of the gloomy front room was a square table covered with a lace cloth on which stood an enormous domed bird cage which was occupied by Archibald, the parrot.

As soon as we trooped in, Archibald hopped from his perch to the bars of his cage where he clawed his way up and down, hanging sideways, or sometimes upside down, screeching obscenities at us. This was one of the major reasons we came to visit - to hear the parrot swear.

'Bugger me! Bugger me!' he would screech - and much, much worse.

Mick started barking but a sharp tap on the nose brought him to order and he sat, with his head on one side, watching the parrot with suspicious awe, while we laughed ourselves silly. Then Ben brought us peanuts in their shells to feed the parrot. All went well until Archibald, less familiar with Peter than he was with me, gave him a sharp nip on the finger. His eyes filled but he managed not to cry.

'Let's have a look,' Ben said and he took Peter's finger and put it in his mouth. He sucked it for a moment and said: 'There, that's better, isn't it?'

Peter looked at his finger and then smiled.

'Magic,' said Ben.

Soon I said that we'd better be going and Ben produced a bowl containing Black Jack chews.

'You can have four each,' he said.

Finally, he performed his party trick. He removed the eye-patch and exposed the eye socket. He had once told me he had a glass eye but was more comfortable without it. Then, he produced two shiny half crown coins and put them inside the socket.

Peter had never seen this before and looked on in horror. I, who had seen it, wanted both to look away and look at the same time. The naked bone inside the socket was deeply shocking. To make matters worse, Ben then held out the two coins to us.

We shook our heads. Two and six each was a fortune. How many Black Jacks would that buy? How many stamps at Stanley Gibbons on Darwen Street? How many trips to the swimming baths? What mountains of chips? But we couldn't accept them. Not after they had been in *there*. We left ruefully and Ben pocketed his money laughing.

What modern parents would have made of Ben doesn't bear thinking about. A man who invited small boys into his house, gave them (or me at least) access to books on the occult, offered them sweets and money, would have become an instant pariah. We were innocents, of course, and no thought of danger ever crossed our minds. Ben was well-known and trusted and I knew that he would sometimes join my dad for a pint at the Whalley Range pub at the top of Brookhouse. Even now, I think he was just lonely.

Once outside again, Mick harassed some pigeons while I explained my plan to Peter. Opposite Ben's house was Boyle Street, known to locals as 'The Bottom' (as opposed to 'The Tops' - open fields up the steep slope of Earl Street in the other direction, where we would make daisy chains and dandelion clocks). The Bottom ran alongside the Brookhouse Mills for about a quarter of a mile before it came to a dead end. Between the street and the works ran the River Blakewater.

It's not what most people would call a river. Its course was pretty ugly at that point, just a sluggish brook or burn, running along a culvert with wide cobbled banks on either side. All the same, it gave its name to the town. Some say it means 'black water' and others 'clear water' from the Old English word *blæc*. I learnt this from one of Ben's books. It was rarely clear when I was a kid. Sometimes it would be a livid green or a bright purple as a result of dyes released from the factories along its course through the town.

Today, as we leaned over the low wall, it was as clear as it ever was. It must have been raining heavily up on the moors over Knuzden way because the brook had overflowed the culvert onto the cobbles. It looked like an elongated puddle.

'We can follow it upstream,' I said to Peter. 'I looked at a map in the Library. We might be able to get as far as Whitebirk. It'll be incredible. We can get over here.' I indicated a point on the low wall.

Peter was as keen as I was but Mick proved a bit of a problem. Peter climbed over the wall first and I handed him over. He had been barking and wriggling with excitement but now he seemed to realise the need to be calm although his tail was whirring like a whisk. I followed them over.

The next bit was tricky. There was a metal ladder down to the cobbles and the river but it was too long for Mick to be handed down. There was only one thing for it: he would have to jump.

I went down first and called to him. He made a couple of tentative efforts but remained on the edge, quivering.

'You'd better come down as well,' I shouted to Peter. 'He won't want to be left behind.'

Peter climbed down and Mick began whining and running up and down the ledge above. I held my arms out.

'Come on, Mick. Come on, boy,' I coaxed. 'You can do it. Come on, boy!'

And, with a literal leap of faith, he landed in my arms. I set him down and he zoomed off barking rapturously, before running back to us.

The Northern Elements

It was weird down here, way below street level. On one side was the sheer brick wall down which we had just climbed. Dark stains showed a high water mark indicating that the river reached surprising levels when in flood. Even darker stains showed the outlines of sheds and penthouses, long since demolished. On the other side of the brook were the massive walls of the mills, covered with filthy windows. Rank weeds grew up the sides and straggling plants with pink flowers hung from crannies in the brickwork. Here and there were doorways leading out to nothing. One of these was open, because of the heat no doubt, and we could see the yellow lights in the roof of the shop floor above us and hear the deafening rattle of the spinning frames. We started to walk upstream along an industrial canyon.

Before long we came to the enclosed bridge which reached above us from the factory to the Bottom. It was black with grime and looked very strange from this angle, slightly exotic even. The door on Boyle Street was always locked - except that once, tired of playing the street games the local girls tried to involve us in - I had wandered off alone and found it open. I heard the girls singing:

> *She is handsome, she is pretty,*
> *She is the girl of the Silver City;*
> *She is counting, one, two, three...*

That usually ends with them trying to snog us, I thought with disgust. This was miles better. There appeared to be no-one about so I crept up the steps and onto the bridge, which I could see was made of wood. Through the grimy windows I could see the Blakewater, which seemed to be in a chasm, miles below.

At the other end I stepped into what appeared to be a store-room piled high with bales of some kind. At the far end there were rubber doors with windows in them, through which you could drive a fork-lift truck without bothering to stop and open them. I could hear the thumping of heavy machinery and a high-pitched whine.

The bale closest to me had had a corner ripped open. Inside was a strange substance. It looked soft and silky, like golden hair. I put my hand in up to the wrist to feel it and the texture was much coarser than I had expected. Just then there was a bang on the leather doors and I could see the prongs of a truck coming through, laden with wooden pallets. I disappeared across the bridge before anyone could see me.

Later my hand began itching really badly. I showed Dad and told him about my exploring.

'It was probably jute,' he said. 'It'll clear up itself.'

All the same he found some calamine lotion and swabbed it over my hand.

'If you're that desperate to get a look around the mill, I'll take you round one day. Might make you work harder at school if you see where you could end up.'

I nodded but what I was really thinking was that there was no point in going round the factory if it was *allowed*. Grown-ups can be really thick sometimes. And I was also thinking that there was no way I was going to end up working in the mill.

1890 THE FERRYMAN

GEORGE SAT ON THE BANK and watched them, chewing the end of a stem of grass. On the far bank, the ferryman sat, tending several fishing rods at once, propped on forked sticks. Beside him, a fire sent up a plume of blue smoke. George waved to him and he waved back.

'What've you got a fire for in this hot weather?' George shouted above the chuckling of water over a little weir a few yards upstream.

'If you're so hot, why aren't you in the water?' the ferryman shouted back.

'He can't swim,' James shouted. He was lying on his back on the surface of the water, kicking furiously with his legs to splash the others.

'Is that right?' the ferryman shouted to George.

'I never learned,' George shouted, as if he were eighty-three and full of a lifetime of regrets.

'You'll have to come over here then if you want to know what the fire's about, won't you?'

'How can I? Are you thick or summat?' George stood up and put his hands on his knees to shout across the river, as if this would add to the force of what he was saying. 'I've already told you I can't swim!'

'I'll have to come and get you then, won't I?' bellowed the ferryman, laughing.

'I haven't any money,' George cried.

'We can pay you, Mister!' Danny shouted from where he was sunning himself on the rocks.

'Yon's too little for me to take a fare,' said the ferryman and the swimmers watched as he checked his lines and then climbed into his boat and took up the broad oars. He rowed in a diagonal where the water was clear and rock-free and Danny was fascinated to see that, at one point, he pointed his prow upstream. An underwater current swung it round again so that, by the time the boat had passed beyond its force, it was travelling in the true direction toward the opposite side.

Wildly excited, George ran along the bank to meet the boat and climbed in. He sat in the stern and gazed up at the ferryman, who turned the boat around, and returned to the north bank.

He was a big man with a big nose and eyes lined with smiles. He wore the coarse blue smock that had been worn by country people for centuries, moleskin trousers and a leather cap. George watched him row with something akin to worship.

When they were about half way across, the ferryman saw that James was stepping over the extreme point of the flat rocks which reached from the south bank more than halfway across the river. He stepped gingerly in order to avoid slipping on algae. He was clearly heading for a bigger pool of still water further downstream.

'Don't go down there!' the ferryman called.

'Why not?' James replied.

'It's dangerous.'

'Bollocks. It's as still as a looking-glass.'

'Aye, on the surface it is but there's powerful undercurrents below. You'll be cut to bits on the rocks.'

'Nah, you're making it up.'

'Do as he says!' Danny shouted.

'It's not his river!' James cried.

'No, but he knows the currents,' Danny replied.

'There were a lad from the college,' the ferryman said, 'not above two year ago, who dived into that stretch from about where you are now, Ginger. They recovered his body down at Ribchester. It was so cut and torn that the authorities were hard put to identify it.'

James turned away from them all to look again at the lower pool.

'DO AS HE SAYS!' Danny all but screamed.

James turned back, but his face was like thunder. He plunged back into the water where the other boys were.

At length, they all climbed out of the water and sunbathed for a while on the southern bank. They had seen the ferryman show George how to check his fishing lines and at one point he had knelt behind Georgie and let the little boy reel in a silvery fish under his guidance. Georgie's face was ecstatic. The ferry-man unhooked the fish, lifted a keep net out of the water, threw

64

George's fish into it, where there were already several others, and man and boy resumed their watch over the lines.

Soon the boys, now dry in the sunshine, reached among their clothes and pulled out their haversacks. They had bought meat pies and each had made sandwiches: jam, meat paste, or just sugar. They shared everything out equally.

'George,' Daniel shouted, 'you've to come back and have your dinner. Can you bring him back, Mister?'

'It's all right, Danny,' George replied. 'I'm having me dinner with Bert. You can have mine.'

He watched as the ferryman took fish, one by one, from the keep net, banged their heads on a stone, swiftly gutted them and threw the guts into the water. Then he laid the fish onto a flat stone which had been placed over the top of the fire hours ago. While the fish baked on the hot stone he went upstream a little to where the water ran fast over the little weir and filled an old military canteen with cold fresh water. Then he fed dry twigs under the baking stone to maintain the heat and from time to time he turned the fish over. The skin crackled and seared and George thought the smell was wonderful.

When the fish was ready, the ferryman produced a loaf of coarse bread from his knapsack and cut thick slices from it. He slid flesh from the bones of the fish onto a slice and gave it to George to eat and George thought he had never tasted anything so blissful.

On the other side of the river, George's friends were enjoying their own feast. There was more than enough for everyone. It's true that some of the sandwiches were better than others but the meat pies had a savoury jelly and the lads were awash with dandelion and burdock. All the same, although they said nothing, each of them was envious of George with his new friend and his hot fish dinner.

'Do you want some?' The ferryman called to the watching boys.

'Are you serious?' Danny replied.

'No,' the ferryman laughed. 'There's only enough for me and Georgie. I never learnt the trick with five barley loaves and two fishes. I'm just the ferryman.'

The boys took his taunt in good part. Richard held up a pair of huge oranges he had stolen from the outdoor market that morning when the stall holders had been setting up their stalls.

'You haven't got any of these though, have you?'

The ferryman laughed and, reaching into the pockets of his smock, he produced two apples which he held up in mockery of Richard. He passed one to George who waved it about and pulled his tongue out at the others. Richard peeled the oranges and doled out the segments. It was all very good-natured. James shook his head at the offer and Richard said:

'Suit yourself - all the more for the rest of us.'

James had been sulking ever since Danny had shouted at him.

After eating, they bathed again and then dried and dozed in the sunshine as the afternoon wore on. They were jolted out of their daydreams by the thud of Bert's boat against the little jetty on their side of the river.

'There's a young man here says you've come from Blackburn,' the ferryman said. 'I think it's probably time you took him home. Summat tells me he's had quite an adventure today and that he's tired.'

'Thanks for looking after him, Bert,' said Danny.

'It's nowt,' said the ferryman. 'I couldn't see him getting bored wi' nowt to do while you lads were larking in the water. Besides, he's kept me entertained. It's a lonely job sometimes, is this, I can tell you. Mind you, he don't half rattle on.'

'Thanks, Bert,' said George.

'Safe journey, kid,' said the ferryman.

The boys gathered their things and set off back. At the top of the ridge, between the trees, where they had first caught sight of the river, they turned to wave and call goodbye. But the ferryman was halfway across and did not turn.

The return walk was quite hard since it was mostly uphill. At first, George rabbited away about how lucky they were to have the place to themselves. The boys of Stonyhurst College were on vacation or they'd have driven the town boys away. There were no masters crossing to intercept a coach on the turnpike road and no farmers going the other way to take supplies up to the

Eagle and Child and the Punchbowl and the Shireburn Arms in Hurst Green.

He soon tired, however, and Rob had to lift him onto his shoulders, where he fell asleep, his arms locked around Rob's forehead and Rob's arms locked around his legs.

They trudged on until the declining sun threw long shadows of trees across the corn stubble and the pungent scent of wild garlic and of honeysuckle filled the air. George dreamt of his friend, the ferryman, and each boy, in his own way, reflected on the finest day of his life so far.

It was dark by the time they reached the Wilpshire tram stop and there was a chill in the air. There was no moon and the lamp by the stop was feeble. That and the faint glow from the railway station below was all the light there was. It was also silent apart from a dog barking far off. The tram was an age and it was a relief when they heard the clang of its bell and it sailed towards them like a galleon, both decks brightly lit.

Though they were exhausted, the boys were profoundly happy. George slept on Rob's shoulder, protected by the big boy's sheltering arm. The others stretched out full length on the wooden benches.

Perhaps faint shadows from the future fell across their happiness. In another week, they would be back at school. By the end of the year, they could be working in one of the mills or factories, doing the same work, day in and day out, for the rest of their lives, in the soot-blackened town.

1960   RATS

ANYWAY, HERE WE WERE walking underneath the black bridge. I imagined we were in a deep ravine in the jungle with a rickety walkway up near the sky, but I didn't tell Peter in case he laughed at me. But there really was a sensation of being deep down. The blackened gables of factory buildings reached down to the river bank. Pipes stuck out from their bricks and would pour their effluent onto the cobbles to seep into the brook. Every so often, there would be a gap between the buildings. At the top of the brick wall, which ran with water, there would be a line of rough palings, held together with wire, and we guessed that factory yards lay beyond.

On our side now there were the gable ends of houses with high chimney stacks, some of them leaning precariously. The Y-shape of rusty drainpipes ran from the gutters on either side. Every now and then, there was a struggling tree, trapped between dark buildings, which seemed to want to crush it and deny it light and air. And every so often, we would come across a buttress, holding up the bulging brick. These triangular structures were made of damp and dripping wood and were often decorated with strange and horrible fungi with frilly orange trumpets of slime.

'Poisonous,' Peter observed quietly.

'Definitely,' I said.

69

Why we were talking in whispers wasn't clear. We only knew that we were privileged to be in this awesome place and that adults wouldn't approve.

We could see that up above us, it was bright and sunny, whilst down here we moved in a world of gloom. In fact, I reckoned that it was several degrees colder down here. At length we came to a little weir beside a small reservoir. This was exciting. Who would have thought that this rather pleasant little spot existed beneath the town, invisible because of high walls above us?

I had done my map reading in the Library pretty thoroughly and was able to tell him that the bridge we had just passed under was at Bastwell, near St Michael and All Angels, where we had both been christened. The healthier looking trees which we soon saw high up on our right must have been in the grounds of the convent - the Convent of the Sisters of Notre Dame it said on the map. This secret world stretched from the fork of the old and new roads to Whalley and was bounded on the far side of the triangle by the river we were following. How so vast a space could exist in the middle of an industrial town was a mystery to me. I would have loved to explore it but the wall down here was unscalable and the walls at street level were high and topped with broken glass. Besides this was RC territory and subject to an unspoken taboo.

Gradually the sunless ravine through which we had been travelling seemed to brighten up a bit. The culvert was still narrow but the walls on either side seemed lower and farther apart. We passed through a short tunnel and when we emerged, there were green banks on either side.

Mick, who had been trotting rather glumly by our side, suddenly zoomed off up the bank on an ecstatic sniffing expedition.

'Do you know where we are?' I said to Peter. Just in front of us and way, way above us were the arches of a railway viaduct.

'I think so,' he said. 'Just coming into Little Harwood. We were up there yesterday, right?'

He pointed up to street level.

'Right,' I said. 'We've just come under Cob Wall Bridge but we're going to fork right now along St. Stephen's Rec. and then there's a really long tunnel which will take us to Whitebirk. Are you game?'

'I'm game,' he said, but he was not convincing.

This expedition was not a new idea. I had proposed it before when Peter had still been the leader. He had vetoed it.

'Why not?' I'd said.

'Rats,' he'd said. 'That's why not.'

And he told us about the danger of rats flitting.

'What's "rats flitting"?' William had asked.

'Well, you know when you move house, it's called "flitting" - well, rats do it an' all,' Peter said.

'Get lost,' William said. 'Rats don't have houses.'

71

'Aye, but if there's a disturbance where they live,' said Peter, 'like building works or summat, they flit somewhere else. Loads of them - hundreds - all together. Like a river of rats.'

'My grandad told me about that,' said Dennis. 'He were a parcel boy before the First World War. They came down Montague Street and there was a white rat leading them and they were in an arrow shape - masses of them - down to King Street Brook. Nothing would stop them - they went over walls and everything. My grandad had to climb up the base of a gas lamp to avoid them.'

'If you corner them, they go straight for your throat,' said Turdy Brown, grabbing hold of William by the neck and pretending to bite him.

'Get off me,' William protested. He was clearly rattled by these stories.

'My mum saw a flitting when she were a little girl, Peter said. 'She lived off Copy Nook and saw them crossing the canal. She said they formed bridges with their bodies so that the little'uns could cross to the other side.'

'They have fleas,' said Turdy. 'That's where the Black Death came from,' and he grabbed William and pretended to pluck imaginary fleas from his hair and eat them.

'Leave me alone will you, you soft sod!' William said, wriggling to get away.

'They say you're never more than six feet away from a rat,' Turdy said, with his face close up to William's.

'I'm going home,' said William. 'I hate you lot!' And he ran off.

'And that's why we're not going down the brook,' Peter had said.

There were a number of reasons why he had been persuaded to come today. One: I was the leader now. Two: he couldn't lose face after I'd completed the triple dog dare and climbed the chimney. Three: there would only be the two of us and we were best mates. Four: I said we'd have the dog with us. And five: because he really wanted to and he would not be the one to be responsible if anything went wrong.

All the same, the old conversation about the flitting rats must have been in both of our minds as we approached the mouth of the tunnel. We had been through a couple of tunnels already but they were quite short and each time we could see the light at the other end perfectly clearly. This tunnel was much longer, if the map in the Library was up to date, and probably went some way underground. As we reached the mouth, we could see that the inside resembled an enormous pipe, with the narrow river running towards us along the bottom.

We could hear the occasional car on Phillips Road and the muted cry of kids playing on the rec. We looked at each other and grinned. There could be no turning back now - it had become a matter of honour.

I had brought a torch with me and its beam seemed to grow brighter as the light from the tunnel mouth lessened. It decreased quite abruptly as we took a bend and soon it was just a dim glow and we could no longer see the entrance if we turned around. The sound of running water echoed everywhere and dirty water dripped from the roof. We didn't speak but pressed on. Mick trotted beside us, staying close. I could sense that he was not too keen about this but he was loyal.

After a while, I thought we had gone beyond the reach of natural light and switched off the torch just to check.

'What the hell are you doing?' Peter cried, and then: 'Oh, Christ! ...'

I had switched the torch back on and the beam immediately hit a writhing knot of rats. They appeared to be fighting over something, tugging it this way and that with their teeth. I saw a flash of red like meat and the gleam of bone and their eyes were tiny points of light as they turned to look at us.

Suddenly Mick began to bark and ran at them.

'No, Mick, no!' I shouted.

At the noise of my shouting and Mick's barking, the rats abandoned the sorry bit of flesh they had been devouring, and slithered, one by one, in no very great hurry, to swim upstream.

I wasn't staying to watch. We turned and fled, me shouting, 'Leave them, Mick. Come on! Come on boy!' And in a couple of moments, he overtook us and bolted ahead.

We did not stop until we had run up the grass bank near the viaduct and Peter had vaulted the low wall. I passed Mick over to him and climbed over myself. We both stood, hearts pounding, with our backs to the wall until we had recovered our breath.

'What do you think it was?' Peter said.

'What do I think what was?' I said.

'What they were eating? It was horrible.'

'I dunno. Another rat? A dead cat?'

'I should bloody well hope it *was* dead!' Peter said and we started laughing and making retching noises. Mick shook himself and barked.

We tramped back to my house. I am willing to bet we were both thinking the same thing - how we would tell the others about our heroic exploits and how we defeated an army of rats.

Back home, we found my father doing some kind of dad-thing with a tin bath in the back yard.

'Anything to eat, Dad?' I asked.

'You've not long had your tea,' he said.

'That was hours ago,' I said. 'I'm starving.'

'There's fruit in the bowl. And there's bread and jam. You're a bottomless pit, you are. And I suppose I'm expected to feed him an' all?'

'Yes please, Mr Catlow,' Peter said.

'Go on, then.'

In the kitchen, we cut ourselves doorsteps of bread and slathered them with butter and strawberry jam. Mum worked evenings or we wouldn't have got away with it. Holding the butties in the flat of our palms, jam uppermost so that it didn't dribble down our sleeves, and nibbling at the corners, we went back into the yard.

'Got enough there, have you?' Dad said.

I ignored his sarcasm.

'What are you doing, Dad?' I said.

'What does it look like? I'm catching a bus.'

'No really.'

'Really? I'm making rhubarb wine.'

I could see that the bath was full of chopped rhubarb over which he had poured masses of sugar and was now adding boiling water.

'Can we have some?'

'It has to ferment before it's done. It'll take months. Should be ready for Christmas, I reckon.'

I'd forgotten about the rhubarb wine long before then.

On New Year's Eve, my parents threw a party. All of our neighbours came along and everyone tried the famous rhubarb wine. I was offered some but thought there was something funny about the smell. Instead, Peter and I got drunk under the table on some stolen port.

I remember two remarkable things about New Year's Day, 1961. I learnt from The Beano that if you turned the comic upside down, the date still read '1961'. That, and the reports that came in, from up and down Brookhouse Lane, of cases of diarrhoea.

1890   SCHOOL

THE LAW SAID that children, between the ages of five and ten, had to be at school. Parents with means might keep their children at school until they were fourteen. Rich parents would, of course, send their boys to public school, where they would continue to be educated until they were young men. They might then go on to university. The daughters of rich parents would be educated at home.

Most of the children of the poor left at the age of ten. Their parents needed the extra money that the children could earn in the factories.

This was the shadow that fell across the happiness of the older boys after their magical day at the Dinkley Ferry. Most boys from poor families were inured to the fact - it was their lot in life - no point in kicking against the traces.

Richard Clayton was not having it. Just occasionally a boy might be noticed as having exceptional academic talent. If parents agreed he might be kept on and educated further, taken out of his class and educated by the Headmaster himself, up to the age of fourteen. Even more rarely, he might be prepared, between the ages of ten and eleven, to sit for an entrance scholarship to the Grammar School which had recently moved from Bull Meadow up to a site near the park. It had been founded by Queen Elizabeth the First for the children of the poor, although nowadays it mostly served the middle classes. All the same, there were a few scholarships for poor boys, funded by philanthropic gentlemen with mutton chop whiskers.

Richard was determined to get one of those scholarships. His father was a senior clerk with the Gas Board but even so he earned less than the mill workers. On the other hand, he was prudent. While the men, and often the women, who worked in the factories would blow their money on the days after pay day, living in spartan poverty later in the week. Mr Clayton was able to put a little by each week. He knew of his son's ambitions. Even if Richard won a scholarship, there would be expenses, and he did not want his son to be despised by the sons of the middling sort.

Winter came and was not kind to the north-west of England. Late September brought gales which stripped the trees bare, weeks before their usual time. There were fogs in October and early November, so thick that you could barely see your feet as you tracked your way to work or school by following the pavement and kerbs. There were blizzards in December and the soft snow drifted so that when Robert woke up one morning there was a bank of snow reaching almost to the top of the front window downstairs. It was so cold that frost had created beautiful ice patterns on the inside of the window. All the same, there was work and school and Rob helped his dad dig a way out through the back yard, where the snow was only calf-high.

Heating was a constant worry for the poor. Sometimes they had to tighten their belts and be even thriftier with food in order to be able to afford to heat one small room. Even then, as you huddled round the fire in the range, your back would be freezing. Women would beg butchers for scraps and bones for soup. Tripe and offal could be made to go a long way. Men might be forced to make sacrifice of a chair, chopping it up for fuel. Boys were sent to see if they could pick up coal along the railway lines. Trespassing on the railway was a serious criminal matter, but what could you do?

But that lay ahead. A week after the idyll in the countryside the boys were back at St. Martin's, their school. It had a girls' entrance at one end, a boys' entrance at the other, and a flagpole on top. The Union Jack was run up on royal birthdays but the Queen had so many relatives it seemed to be up there most of the time.

The inside was bleak. The windows were high so that the children would not be distracted from their rounds of rote learning by anything going on outside. The sparse natural light was supplemented by yellow gas lamps, winter and summer alike. The walls were bare, apart from framed texts such as:

CLEANLINESS IS NEXT TO GODLINESS
SUFFER THE LITTLE CHILDREN TO COME UNTO ME
SPARE THE ROD AND SPOIL THE CHILD
I AM THE WAY THE TRUTH AND THE LIFE
GOD IS LOVE

79

The children worked at desks which had a built-in wooden seat and a lid - books were kept inside. Each unit was for two children and had two ceramic ink wells. The desks were bolted to the floor so that there was no shifting and scraping of chairs and there was minimum space for fidgeting. Girls sat on one side of the classroom and boys on the other. Villains sat on the front row where they could be knuckled on the head or tapped sharply by the edge of the teacher's ruler. Boffins sat at the back because they could be trusted.

Richard sat somewhere near the middle but he was resolved that this year he would cut down on his truancy and also the thieving. It would ruin his plans entirely if ever he were caught. He had already been 'noticed' for his academic ability and had been made a monitor, as had James. Monitors were children who were given a specific task to help out the teacher. James, for instance, was ink monitor. He had to make sure that all the ink wells were topped up. The ink was delivered in powder form and had to be mixed with tap water in a large enamel jug usually with a yard-long ruler which had no other purpose. This was not easy and there was a tendency for little clots of undissolved ink powder to accumulate near the bottom of the jug. For this reason, James would fill his own inkwell first, then Mr Bamford's (who was otherwise known as Concrete Head) and so on, down through a hierarchy of his own devising, with Daniel last. James was still sulking at him for the rebuke down at Dinkley.

The dip pens the older children used were little more than a wooden stem (often chewed ragged at the end) and a nib. If the nib picked up a little ink clot it could cause a blot in your copy book and this was a punishable offence. James was hoping that this would happen to Daniel. It would be a wonderful revenge to see him made to stand in the corner, or get the ruler or, best of all, beaten on the bum by Concrete Head's whippiest cane.

Nothing divided Miss Hick's class of younger children from the bigger schoolroom but a dusty curtain which could be drawn back to combine the two classes for morning worship. Often the older children would be distracted from multiplying pounds, shillings and pence by the younger ones chanting their times tables. George was in Miss Hicks's class.

Richard was altar monitor. Because St Martin's was a church school, much time was given over to prayers and study of the Bible. Richard was allowed in from the playground before the others to draw back the curtain. The desks in both school-rooms would now face Mr Bamford's desk, which stood on a dais. From a cupboard Richard would take a white table cloth, washed and ironed weekly by Miss Hicks, and over it he would lay a smaller cloth of purple velvet (purple was for repentance, they were often told). A plain wooden cross on a simple plinth was placed in the centre and on either side, pewter candlesticks with tall church candles. Now - and this shows how much

Richard was trusted - he would take a box of matches from a drawer in the desk and light the candles. Finally, he would lift a plain wooden lectern, which stood in a corner by day, onto the dais, next to the altar.

Then the children would be lined up in the playground by Mr Bamford and admitted in silence to their classrooms. Miss Hicks would be seated at the piano and Mr Bamford would go to the Headmaster's office to tell him that all was ready. All would stand as the Head, in gown and mortar board, took his place at the lectern and Concrete Head would remain with his back to the door as if to prevent anyone escaping.

They would sing a hymn: 'Eternal Father, Strong to Save' was a favourite. They liked the minor key melodrama of the middle section of each verse although Mrs Hicks's jangly piano seemed to be striving somehow to make it sound jolly. Then the Head would deliver a sermon. These could be up to half an hour long and all the time Concrete Head would be scanning the rows of pupils for signs of drowsiness or inattention.

They rarely saw the Head apart from these assemblies. He was a crook-backed, hooked-nosed little man with tufts of hair bristling in his ears and nostrils and a sharp, acidic voice. His constant message was that, although they were born worthless, with industry they could attain to great things. Why, he, himself, he never tired of telling them, had been a student at All Souls, Oxford. Worship would end with lengthy prayers.

The children had no way of knowing that he was lying: All Souls does not admit undergraduates. Little George could do a hilarious impression of him, however, gathering an imaginary gown behind him and clasping his hands. Strutting about, he would say: 'Now then - Limbs of Satan - fine school - esteemed colleagues - Miss Hicks - fine woman - Robert Catlow - you'll go far - might as well leave now - I, myself, am a bloody genius - went to Poxford, y'know - Arseholes College...'

George's swearing was coming on a treat.

The rest of the morning was 'Scripture' or Bible Study. Some of the battles in the Old Testament were all right, and Jesus's miracles were good, along with the spooky appearances after the Resurrection. Some of the parables were a bit puzzling though. Why did the Prodigal Son get the fatted calf when he was a lazy article and the other brothers had done well with their money? And why did Jesus blast the fig tree? What had it ever done to him? It didn't do to ask Concrete Head these questions - or any questions at all for that matter.

Rob had found this out last January when they were studying Luke's gospel and he had innocently asked what 'circumcise' meant. Concrete Head had beaten him savagely but gave him no answer. Danny and Richard were so angry about the injustice of this that they took Robert down to the Reading Room in the Library to look it up in the dictionary. They found it in the A-D volume and were promptly thrown out for laughing, and clutching their privates with both hands and making 'eeuw' noises.

The afternoons were for the three R's: Reading, wRiting and aRithmetic. Lessons were mostly a question of copying from the blackboard and learning by rote. Phenomenal feats of mental arithmetic were expected and failure meant the stool in the corner and the pointed cap with 'D' for dunce written on the front. Handwriting was expected to be uniform - in the cursive copperplate style - the capital 'H' was a nightmare. You were supposed to write it without taking your pen off the page but there were so many loops in it that you risked your nib running out of ink before you could complete it.

In George's class, the children used slates with a slate pencil. Their work could be rubbed out. Paper was very expensive and the younger children were more liable to mistakes so this was a practical economy. George hated Writing and would often end up in tears. He was left-handed but Miss Hicks forced him to use his right hand by tying his left behind his back to the metal frame of the desk unit. If his letters were a mess, as was usually and inevitably the case, he would be punished for it. Miss Hicks was as dried up as a vanilla pod.

There was no art, no music, no drama and no literature apart from the Bible. The school day ended at five o'clock in the afternoon.

1961   HOLY DOG

THE CLOCKS HAD CHANGED and the evenings were getting lighter. We would dawdle on our way home from school, staving off pre-teatime hunger pangs with a visit to the sweet shop on the corner of Shear Brow. We would go for Black Jacks, kali and spanish, Sherbet Fountains, Flying Saucers, Cherry Lips and Lucky Bags. None of this did us any harm: we were active, we walked or ran everywhere - to and from school, uphill and down - and we ranged the town and the fields and moors whenever we were let off the leash.

Sometimes we would go into town after school, perhaps to the Library where I had only recently been promoted to the adult section and where I was working my way through the Sherlock Holmes stories. Sometimes we would condescend to return to the children's Library and help Willie to choose a Dr Seuss book. *Green Eggs and Ham* came out that year and Willie learnt large chunks of it by heart. On the wall of the Children's Library was a print of *The Carnival of Harlequin* by Joan Miró. We didn't know that at the time, of course, and we certainly knew nothing of Dada or surrealism. We were fascinated by its weirdness and its energetic colours. We didn't bother ourselves with what it meant. Willie told us stories about it with absolute conviction: stories about the pipe-smoking wizard and his mechanical cat and how they rid the kingdom of flying snakes with help of a magic guitar.

Peter and Turdy had sisters and sometimes they would tag along when we went into town, whether we wanted them to or not. Usually, the consensus was 'not'. Peter's sister, Ann, was a sly nine-year old with pigtails. Turdy's sister, Jean, was only seven, and would declare, to Willie's horror, that she was in love with him and was going to marry him.

Girls were a different species, not as strange as Roman Catholics, or grown-ups, or people from Yorkshire, but alien all the same.

The girls would play skipping games, either individually or with a long rope, chanting various nonsensical verses; the boys would play football (though I was not keen), with coats and jumpers as goal posts, or rounders (much better), or a rough version of tennis or cricket. The boys were travellers and explorers; the girls sat on doorsteps nursing their dolls. They collected scraps: these were cut-out, highly coloured paper images in relief of Victorian children, flowers, fruit and cherubs (children's heads - mostly girls, mostly curly) over a pair of coloured wings. These came in various sizes and the girls collected them in shoe boxes and the like and swapped them like a kind of currency. We boys collected stamps.

If the girls became a nuisance, Peter had an infallible way of getting rid of them. Upstairs in the Library building were art galleries and museums. There was an Egyptian mummy in one of the rooms in a glass case. Peter would get the girls to stare at it, without blinking, and then suddenly say: 'It moved!' The girls would rush out shrieking hysterically and the elderly attendant would glare at us. We would just shrug at him as if to say: 'Girls, eh? What do you expect?'

Thing is, it worked every time. And not just with the mummy. One room was given over to Victorian taxidermy. Peter would lead the girls to a glass case where, in a miniature landscape, a stoat was creeping up on an unsuspecting rabbit. They would stare and stare until Peter said: 'it moved' and the girls would scream to order.

A case of stag beetles, including one colossal specimen, would bring on hysteria without any help from Peter.

Frightening the girls was a brilliant game. But there came a time when the girls didn't want to play any more. They began to hang about with a bunch of older girls and collect photos of pop stars which came with packets of bubble gum and toffee fags. They would drool over Elvis and Cliff and Billy Fury and Bobby Vee and Adam Faith and the Everly brothers. To us, this was in- comprehensible and, to be honest, a bit weird.

One day, Peter announced that he was going to scare the rest of us instead.

'What are you going to do?' said Willie. 'Show us your bum?'

'It's a good match for your face, you cheeky wazzock!'

'What are you going to do then?' said Dennis.

'Not telling you yet,' Peter said. 'You'll see. But it's to do with the Rednecks.'

'Rednecks' was our nickname for Roman Catholics. Catholic kids on our street called us Proddy-dogs. In truth there was no real animosity between the two groups of kids and we would often mix freely in our games down the Bottom. Likewise, with our parents, the division didn't run particularly deep. My mother would sometimes whisper about a new family in the area: 'They're Catholics, you know', but would chat happily with the mother in the Co-op. There was irritation at the Catholic objection to marriage outside the faith but, apart from that, the common attitude was a faint shadow of the conflicts of distant times. We knew that the feud was still going on in Ireland but, to us, it was more like the spectre of the Wars of the Roses that survives in the game of grudges you get in cricket matches between Lancashire and Yorkshire.

Daphne and Bernadette were Catholics. Hearing that I was bright they invited me over to their house across the street to listen to a play about Joan of Arc on the wireless.

Well, Sunday afternoons were boring enough, and Mum said: 'Go on, they'll spoil you,' so I went.

You could tell they were Catholics the minute you stepped into their front room. There was a crucifix on the fireplace. In the middle of the room was a round table with a dark blue velvet cover. This was covered with a lace cloth on top of which stood the wireless set and on top of that that there was a large statuette of the Virgin Mary staring up to heaven. It was a sunny day out-side but there was a smoky little fire in the grate and the curtains were half-closed. On the wall, was a picture of Jesus, with much longer hair than I was used to, spread over his shoulders. He looked terribly sad and kind. He was pointing to his own bleed-ing heart which seemed to have rays of light coming out of it. It was like some kind of Martian weapon from a Dan Dare comic. I didn't like it. It was a bit scary.

The play was quite good, but very long. On the other hand, Daphne (or Bernadette) put a bowl of sweets on the table and told me to help myself - I needed no second bidding - and later Bernadette (or Daphne) brought in tea and a scrumptious plum cake.

'They're trying to convert you, you know,' Mum said when I got home.

'Why?' I asked.

'Souls for Jesus,' she said.

'What?' I said, but I'd already lost interest because tea was ready - tinned salmon with salad and hard boiled eggs.

My dog, Mick, was a Roman Catholic. At least, that's what Mum said. And this is how she found out.

Every couple of weeks, we walked in pairs from St John's School to Belper Street Swimming Baths. Our route took us through Brookhouse Lane and my mother would wave to us and sometimes have a little chat with our Headmaster, Mr Nelson. One day, as we reached our street, I could see that Mum was standing on the doorstep talking to a priest. I could tell he was RC because his cassock buttoned down the side rather than down the front like Canon Balderstone at St John's - and he didn't have a dog collar.

'What were you talking about to that priest?' I asked Mum at teatime.

'About Mick.'

'What about Mick?'

'How he must be a Catholic.'

'Why must he be a Catholic?'

'Well, Father Ignatius brought him home because Mick had got into St Urban's and was sitting in there staring up at a statue of the Virgin. He would have sat there for hours if the Father had not decided that it was perhaps a bit disrespectful to the people who wanted to pray there, so he gave him a blessing and brought him home. This is about the fifth or sixth time this has happened, so we reckoned Mick must be a Catholic at heart.'

'He won't be able to marry a Proddy-dog now,' Dad said and guffawed into his pint pot of tea.

We stared at him. He had made a joke. This was rare.

'Anyway,' Mum said. 'He practically begged me to keep Mick at home. "What can you do?" I said. "He mopes about and gets in the way all day till Tommy gets home. And besides, he needs exercise. I haven't the time and besides that's a job *a certain person* promised to do twice a day."'

I could see what was coming and said: 'Please may I leave the table?'

'Help your mother with the washing up,' Dad said, looking over the top of *The Lancashire Evening Telegraph*, 'and then take that dog for a walk.'

'But I said I'd call for Peter and see if he were playing out...'

'No buts,' said Dad from behind the paper.

'Aw, Dad...'

'Never mind "Aw, Dad" - sooner you start, sooner you finish.'

We tossed a coin and I got washing and Mum got drying.

'Right, that's that,' I said at last, wiping my hands on Mum's apron.

''Ere, what about these pans?' Mum said.

'They need to soak!' I shouted back. I was already in the front room, putting Mick's lead on.

'Lazy beggar,' she cried. 'He learned that particular trick from you,' she said to Dad.

I put my head round the living room door.

'Dad,' I said. 'What's a virgin?'

'Go on, get out!' he shouted and threw a slipper in my direction which hit the door.

'Come on, Holy Dog,' I said.

1891   ORPHAN

THIS IS AN EXTRACT from *The Blackburn Standard and Weekly Express* of April 5, 1891:

SUICIDE BY HANGING

An inquest was held on the evening of Wednesday last by the East Lancashire Coroner, at The Dolphin Hotel, Mount Street, Blackburn, touching the death by hanging of Walter Catlow, cotton weaver, at his home on Cambridge Street, on March 27th, being Good Friday. The deceased was twenty-eight years of age.

It appears, from the deposition of his sister-in-law, Elsie Slater, of Maudsley Street, that he had been suffering from a depression of spirits brought on by the death of his wife the previous year and that he had sought solace in drink. A fortnight before his demise, he had turned up for work at the River Street Mill very much the worse for wear and had been summarily dismissed. His employers refused to give him a character and this preyed upon his mind, as he thought he should not be able to obtain any more work.

On the morning before the body of the deceased was discovered, according to the testimony of his ten-year old son, Daniel, he rose early and said that he meant to go looking for work and that he had a mind to walk to Preston and see if any employment might be had there. His instructions were that his son should go to school as usual and then to the house of his aforementioned aunt, Elsie Slater, who would expect him and that he was to spend the night there.

On Good Friday morning, upon visiting his home to ascertain if his father might be returned, he was horrified to find him hanging by a rope from a bacon hook fixed to the ceiling of the kitchen. He ran for his aunt who procured the aid of a neighbour, one Alfred Horrocks, to cut the body down. They raised the alarm but when medical assistance arrived, life was declared extinct.

The Coroner gave notice that no blame appeared to be attached to anyone connected with the deceased and the jury returned a verdict that the deceased had destroyed himself whilst in a state of temporary insanity. In conclusion, the Coroner expressed concern for the welfare of the orphaned boy, whereupon the boy's aunt, Mrs Slater, declared that she would receive the boy into her own home and undertake to raise him as her own.

Heaven knows, she could ill afford this generosity, what with children of her own to rear, but she could not for shame let her poor dead sister's child go upon the parish. Daniel showed no gratitude. For a fortnight, he did not even speak. He just sat by the range, staring at the fire and poking at the coals. The others called to ask if he was playing out yet but he refused even to go to the door.

Elsie had a heart of gold but things were strained. Her husband, Arnie, was a fitter at the Albion Mill out at Ewood. He did his best to accommodate Danny, but he worked long hours, and he had a two-mile walk to and from work each day. And then there were the children. The baby, Lillian, was only six months old, and the twins, Arthur and Ethel, were five, so Elsie had her hands full. She needed to get work but a child minder would have to be found and paid. She had hoped when she took Daniel in that he could, at least, look after the twins but as it was, he was of use to neither man nor beast.

It was true that he was eating next to nothing and was losing weight but she still had to put the food in front of him and was exasperated when, after a few mouthfuls, he pushed away the plate. Money was very tight and waste was sinful.

Baby Lillian slept in a cot in her parents bedroom and Daniel had to share a bed with the other children. Arthur told his mother one day that he couldn't get to sleep for Danny crying. Danny never cried in the day time.

Elsie's compassion was deep - she had her own grief, after all - but things could not go on like this. She could sense that her husband was becoming impatient. She also felt that her own children were a little frightened by Danny's dejection and had become very subdued in his presence.

One night, Danny heard Elsie and Arnie arguing downstairs and he crept out of bed and sat on the stairs to hear what was going on.

'I don't care, Elsie,' his uncle was saying. 'Something has got to change around here.'

'I know Arnie, but he's all broken up inside.'

'But moping about like this isn't going to help him, is it?'

'Give him time.'

'Give him time? Give him time? It's been three weeks and more.'

'Oh, Arnie, love, he's only a bairn.'

'What is he? Ten? He needs to start growing up fast. The world won't wait for him, Elsie. When his mother died, Walter was given the morning off for the funeral and he had to be back at his machine in the afternoon.'

'I'll talk to him.'

'Aye, well it had better be good. When I see my own childer moping about because they're frit of him - well, I'm not having it. You can tell him that he mun buck his ideas up or it's the workhouse.'

'Oh, you wouldn't, Arnie.'

Daniel could hear his aunt crying.

'I don't want to, love, but this mumping about has got to stop. For a start, he has got to get back to school. I'm not having teachers coming to the house and showing us up in front of the whole street.'

Mr Bamford had indeed called round and been given a cup of tea. Danny would not speak to him and went to lie on the bed upstairs. Bamford had shown a wooden sort of sympathy but explained that if Danny did not make a showing at school, the Headmaster would be obliged to inform the Inspectors. This had been a week ago.

'And he needs to be out playing with his friends,' Arnie continued. 'Take his mind off it. And he needs to get some fresh air. He's beginning to look like a corpse himself.'

Their voices dropped then and Daniel couldn't hear what they were saying. He had heard things about the workhouse and he didn't like what he'd heard. He stole back to bed.

The next Saturday, soon after dinner, there was a knock on the door and when Elsie opened it the boys were standing there.

'Is Danny playing out yet?' Richard said.

'I don't know,' Elsie said very tentatively. 'Hang on. I'll see what he says.'

But, when she turned round, Daniel was standing behind her with his coat and cloth cap on.

'Oh, Danny lad!' she said, bending down to kiss him.

'Gerroff!' he said, with ghost of a smile. 'In front of me mates an' all. Honestly.'

'Yeah well. You go off and enjoy yourself,' Elsie said.

'And don't come back till tea-time!' her husband called from the back kitchen.

Over the next few days, Richard found that, although Daniel came out with them whenever they called for him, he was not his old self. Sometimes, you might think he'd made the break-through and he would laugh and joke with you, like the old days. But these occasions were as bright and brief as summer lightning. Often he would be silent, following on behind, as if he had retreated into a different, desolate world. At other times, he would be prickly, flaring into a rage at the least thing.

He left it to Richard to come up with ideas for their play and seemed to prefer James's company, their tiff down by the river now forgotten. The two of them often combined to show their impatience with George's prattling and then they would be so sharp with him that his eyes would fill up.

One day, they were in a back street behind The Wellington Hotel throwing stones at tin cans that they had lined up on a wall. James grew bored and began tormenting a cat that had come along hoping to be petted. James stroked it for a while and then began pulling it about by the tail. Daniel stood by laughing and then grabbed the tail from James and lifted the yowling animal into the air.

'Let it go!' Robert shouted and Danny dropped the cat which went streaking off to safety. 'If I catch either of you pulling off a stunt like that ever again, I swear I'll punch your lights out.'

This was shocking coming from Rob, gentle Rob, who was always so loyal, reserved and uncomplaining. There was no doubt that he could do what he threatened and Daniel and James deferred to his size but Richard felt that this was the beginning of a rift in the gang which it would be hard to repair.

At school, Daniel was sullen and unapproachable. He took no interest in his lessons and he quickly dropped to the bottom of the class. Concrete Head, though not a paragon of sensitivity, was conscious enough of the boy's double bereavement not to put him in the corner with the dunce's hat. On the other hand, he took no interest in him thereafter and offered him no help in his lessons.

One morning at playtime, another boy was foolish enough to call him 'mardy-arse'. Danny began to beat him up so viciously that the other boys were too scared to pull him off his victim. By the time Mr Bamford arrived, the other boy had a bloody face and had lost a tooth.

Bereavement or not, Bamford gave Daniel a severe beating for that but Daniel did not shed a single tear.

1961   STATUES

I HAD BEEN INSIDE ST URBAN'S myself once. The Catholic church
was big, bigger than St John's. It seemed to me to be as big as the
Cathedral, though it probably wasn't. It stood on Larkhill at the
other end of Brookhouse Lane and there was nothing on the
outside to say that it was any different.

One Saturday morning, Turdy Brown and I had been in
town and we decided to come home via Penny Street and
Larkhill for a change. Just before we reached the top of Brookhouse Lane, there was a sudden shower so heavy that you could
barely see ahead of you. Turdy pointed to the doorway of the
Craven Heifer pub but I saw that the door of St Urban's was
open and, as it was nearer, I ran across the road and through the
burial ground with Turdy following.

It was too late, of course. Our clothes were drenched, our
socks squelched in our shoes, water dripped from our hair, there
were rain drops in our eyelashes. As we stood in the porch,
blinking the water away, we could hear a strange chanting that
came from beyond the double doors that led into the church.
Cautiously, we pushed through them and they closed behind us
with a whisper.

It was so different from St John's, which in the daytime was
light and airy and, in the evenings, sort of intimate and safe. This
place was high and gloomy and the stained glass windows so in-

tricate that they didn't seem to admit much light. The altar seemed a long way away and it was very elaborate. There was a lot of gold and several very tall candles and a little red light burned somewhere to the side.

We couldn't see where the chanting was coming from but a rich deep male voice was filling the church. I couldn't make out the words but I guessed it might be Latin. The same words were repeated again and again. From time to time they were mumbled by a few ragged voices in reply. And it went on and on. There was a smell of incense unlike the faintly musty smell of St John's. It was all very strange and spooky.

The biggest difference was the statues which were placed at intervals down both sides of the nave. They were slightly larger than life and they were painted in bright colours. There were prie-dieux in front each of them and racks on which candles were burning. I realised these were statues of saints when I recognised John the Baptist with a lamb under his arm and a little cross at the top of his staff. There was also St Peter with a bishop's mitre and a bunch of keys. I knew this from an illustration in one of Ben's encyclopaedias. I didn't recognise any of the others, except that the last statue on the right, near the chancel steps, was the Virgin Mary all in blue with a gold crown. She had more candles than any of the others put together and the light made her blue robes glow.

In front of her knelt two elderly women, hands clasped together. Perhaps they were the ones who had reported Mick to

Father Ignatius. Suddenly I realised that I knew who they were: Daphne and Bernadette. As I turned to drag Turdy outside with me, I recognised another statue: a girl in white armour carrying a blue flag with white lilies on it - Joan of Arc.

I pulled Turdy through the doors. I didn't actually believe that we would be hauled down into hell fire but there was a strong sense of trespass in our intrusion and I did not want Bernadette and Daphne to see me.

Once outside, the moment of panic vanished. The sun had come out and the rain was steaming off the pavements. We had a bottle of sarsaparilla each at Mrs Wilkinson's and made our way home for our dinner.

The following Saturday the gang met up at the lamp post outside my house. I was going to suggest that we play in the cemetery. There was nothing ghoulish about this - it was just a terrific place to play hide-and-seek. It was built on a hillside and if you looked upwards from the bottom there was a crazy landscape of Victorian gothic spires and crosses and lamenting angels reaching into the sky. Out of respect we always stayed away from any fresh graves near the boundaries or any graves that were being tended.

I sensed that my suggestion was meeting with a lukewarm response. It was true that it was a very hot day and the cemetery was a long trek out along Whalley New Road. The sky was heavy and thundery. I have to say I was a bit miffed when Peter came up with an alternative suggestion. Was this a coup? An attempt to regain his leadership?

'You know I said I were going to scare the pants off the lot of you?'

'I'm not scared of nothing,' said Willie.

'That's a double negative,' said Dennis, who was pedantic as well as practical. 'It means you're scared of something.'

'Get stuffed, specky-four-eyes,' said Willie.

'Or scared of *everything*,' Dennis persisted.

'Shut up, Dennis,' I said. 'Go on, Peter.'

'Well, you know St. Urban's?'

'Oh that,' I said airily. 'Me and Turdy were in there last Saturday. It's spooky an' all but it's not going to put skid marks in our kecks. You'll have to do better than that.'

'No, I don't mean that. There's a road that goes all the way round the back of the church called St. Urban's Place.'

'So what,' I said, 'there's a road that goes to Accrington called Accrington Road.'

'There's a road that goes to Whalley called Whalley New Road,' said Willie.

'Shut up, Willie,' Peter said.

'There's a road that goes to Preston called Preston New Road,' said Willie.

'Yeah, shut up, Willie,' I said. 'What are you getting at Peter?' I'd noticed St Urban's Place. There were big houses there which I assumed were for the priests, but it had never occurred

102

to me to go round the back. It was too much like foreign territory.

'Right. Well, the houses round the back are derelict. You can get in and explore. The roofs have fallen in everywhere but you can get in the rooms - and there are cellars.'

It was the last word that I could feel animating the others - it had the spice of danger about it.

'What do you think, Tommy?' Peter said.

'I don't know,' I said, playing for time. 'It could be dangerous.'

'When has that ever put you off, Tommy Catlow?'

I grinned.

'All right then. Let's go!' I said. 'Last one at the Heifer's a cissy! Hi-yo Silver, away!'

And I galloped off on my imaginary horse, like the Lone Ranger, down Brookhouse Lane to the Bottom, and up the other side to the Craven Heifer. Turdy came last. Even Willie with his little legs beat him. Turdy was big but he was slow.

We crossed the road and into St Urban's Place. On our right was the low wall of the burial ground with a row of gloomy yew trees along the inside. On our left were three storey houses with little untended gardens. Stone steps led up to each dingy front door. They all needed a lick of paint and their brass fittings had turned green long ago. The windows were blank. There appeared to be no curtains. We weren't sure whether the houses were still occupied. Dennis volunteered to go and have a peep but Peter said we were too near the main road and that the houses at the back of the church were definitely empty. We went on.

It was very close. A few fat drops of rain fell and then stopped. Thunder growled in the distance.

Around the bend the houses had only two storeys but longer gardens. It was clear that they were unoccupied. They were ruins with no roofs, as Peter had said. I thought I would assert my leadership and said: 'Wait here.'

The first house had no gate and I walked up the short path. The front door was hanging off its hinges and I went in.

'Not that one, y'idiot!' Peter was shouting. I walked over dust and fallen plaster into a room off the hallway. What I saw made me turn around and run out retching.

'What's the matter?' the others cried.

'I told you not to go in there,' Peter said. 'I've been in them all.'

I ignored him and explained to the others what I had seen. In the corner of the room was a filthy mattress surrounded by empty beer bottles. Here and there on the floor were stinking coils of human excrement.

'Just a tramp,' Peter said.

'Bloody hell!' said Willie. 'Will he come back?'

'Nah,' Peter said. 'Not till dark anyway. This is the house. Come on.'

He led the way through the gate of the middle house which was intact and up to the front door, also intact, although un-locked. We trooped after him. I was annoyed at his taking the lead but what could I do? The others were excited and intrigued.

In this house, not only had the roof gone but the ground floor ceilings too. Through the dust and debris I could see that the vestibule and hallway were paved with beautiful tiles in red and green. There were rooms on either side. In one of them, the beams were still in place, running across the room, and above them a clear view of the sky which was brightening. On the floor lay the joists and the floorboards from the room above, amid a great deal of plaster and dust. On the mantelpiece, above a fire-place with long-cold ashes still in its grate, there was a little cru-cifix, which seemed to be made out of plastic.

'Come here, everybody,' Peter was calling from the hallway and I went out to join the others. Willie was already sitting on the steps of a stairway which led up to nowhere.

'Here we are,' Peter said. He was standing next to the open door under the stairs. 'The cellar's down here.'

I clambered over some rubble to get to him. I could see stone steps going down into the darkness with a metal rail on one side.

'Down you go then,' Peter said. He was grinning. 'If you dare.'

'Oh, I'm not playing double-dog dare games, Peter Shaw-cross,' I said. 'I'm up for it. Willie, you don't have to come if you don't want to.'

'I do want to,' Willie said.

'All right then, stay close to me and keep hold of the rail.'

I began to go down. Willie followed, holding the rail with one hand and clutching my tee-shirt in the small of my back with the other. Then came Turdy. We were about half-way down when a torch beam from above streamed past us and threw our shadows on the flagstones below. Dennis always carried his torch with him.

'No torches,' Peter shouted. 'You're not going to see any ghosts with a torch on, are you?'

'Ghosts?' Willie whimpered behind me.

'There's no such thing, Willie. Don't you worry. Just stick with me,' I said. 'Do as he says, Denny. Turn it off.'

A cloud must have passed over the sky above the house because, when the torchlight went out, it was pitch dark.

Without warning, a hideous illuminated face leapt out of the dark at us. It went out and we were in the dark again. Willie held my hand tightly. Then another face, hideous and brightly coloured, came looming out of the dark at us.

'Jesus!' Turdy muttered behind me. Another face, then darkness, then another. My heart was banging and my legs were like jelly.

106

There was a long pause in the darkness. The after-image of the last face lingered on my retina. Suddenly, another face appeared beside me at Willie's eye level. It was right in front of Willie's face, bright green with hollows for eyes. The hideous gleam lit Willie's face too. Then it turned red.

Willie started screaming hysterically.

A torch snapped on and Dennis sprayed the beam around the cellar. It was immediately clear what had been going on. Peter was crouching in front of Willie holding a torch under his chin. It was one of those that change colour with a flick of a switch. Around the room were plaster statues which had been retired from the church. They were propped up all around the walls of the cellar. Most of them were broken. They had limbs missing. Some were headless. One lacked a nose, another half its face. A bishop had lost a hand and it lay on the floor with his crozier. All of them were garishly painted. Peter had picked out faces with his torch and they had seemed to move in the darkness. Now, in the light of Dennis's torch, they just looked pathetic.

But Willie was not consoled. He ran up the stairs and we could hear him wailing all the way.

'You great dickhead,' I said to Peter. 'Look what you've done.'

'It were only a joke,' Peter shouted after me.

I found Willie sitting on the low wall of the graveyard near the main road, crying his eyes out. He was inconsolable.

The others appeared and stood in front of us, looking gormless, their hands in their pockets. Peter started to speak.

'You'd better go home, you, afore I deck you,' I said.

He sloped off, looking down at the pavement.

'You an' all,' I said to the others more gently. 'I'll sort him out. It's better if it's just me.'

When they'd gone I explained to Willie what Peter had done.

Gradually, his heartbreak subsided to little shuddering sobs.

I said:

Do you like
Green eggs and ham?
I do not like them
Sam-I-am,
I do not like
Green eggs and ham.

Willie laughed. I continued:

Would you like them
Here or there?

Willie took over. I knew he'd learnt lots of it by heart.

The Northern Elements

I would not like them
Here or there,
I would not like them
Anywhere.

Holding his hand, I walked him all the way home to his house on 'Animal' Street.

Neither of us had any idea that another horror awaited us, one far worse than anything that had happened in the cellar, one that would stay with us for the rest of our lives.

1891   CANAL

JAMES'S FASCINATION WITH TRAINS inspired the last adventure before the calamity. Daniel was still the nominal leader of the gang but the ideas came from Richard or James, and Daniel would give his assent with a cursory 'If you want...' or 'Yeah, let's do that.' These days he never even bothered to veto the other boys' plans.

The train ride was the last and only time the gang seemed happy together after the death of Danny's father and even Daniel himself seemed to come out of his shell. James had proposed that they catch the train to Darwen.

'How can we do that? We can't afford tickets,' Richard said.

'We get platform tickets,' James said. 'I think they're only a halfpenny or a penny at most.'

'What are platform tickets?' George asked.

'What are platform tickets?' James mimicked his voice in a sing-song tone. 'Platform tickets, pygmy, are what the nobs buy when they are seeing off their nearest and dearest but are not travelling themselves. You can get on the platform but not on the train.'

'But I thought you said we *were* getting on the train?' George said.

'Bloody Nora,' James said. 'Will somebody please shut him up.'

'Shut up, pygmy,' Danny said, picking up on the insult.

'What's a pygmy?' George asked.

Danny gave him a clunk on the back of the head and George shut up, but stuck out his lower lip.

James continued.

'Now then. We get onto the platform and when the guard isn't looking, we find an empty compartment and get on.'

Trains at the time had no corridors so James's plan seemed at least plausible.

'We might get past the guard but what about the other passengers. Won't they smell a rat?'

'There won't hardly be any other passengers,' James said. 'We'll be going first class!'

The others laughed in disbelief.

'Get out of it,' Richard said. 'How will we manage that?'

'Just use that fat brain of yours, Rich,' James said. 'We're not paying for a travel ticket so what does it matter what class we travel?'

'Fair enough,' said Richard.

'I'm going to be a nob,' George sang out, in what he thought was a posh accent.'

'You're a knob all right,' Danny said. 'Now belt up.'

George thrust his lower lip out to the limit.

'Anyway,' James said, 'it's better if we go first class. We'll be less likely to be noticed.'

'How do you work that out?' Richard asked.

The Northern Elements

'What we do is get the first train in the morning to Manchester. It goes through Darwen and Bolton and it starts from Blackburn so we won't be hanging about on a through platform looking obvious. We get there just on time, walk past the buffers, through the crowds getting on the second and third class coaches, and up to the first class carriage in front of the engine. The toffs don't even get out of bed before ten o'clock so there'll hardly be anybody there. We hop into a first class carriage and Bob's your uncle and Fanny's your aunt.'

George opened his mouth to say his auntie was not called Fanny but Daniel glared at him so he shut it abruptly.

Robert had been thinking about this.

'What about the other end? Won't they check our tickets?' he said.

'Ah, there's the beauty of it,' James replied. 'We don't get off at Darwen station.'

'I thought you said we did,' Rob said.

'I said we were going to Darwen but not to the station. Just before it pulls in, it slows right down to go through the points in the shunting yard. We open the door and jump out. Easy as pie.'

'How do you know all this?' Richard said.

''Cos I've done it,' James said. 'Only I didn't get a platform ticket. I climbed over the fence and went up the platform by the ramp. I hid behind some milk churns until it was time.'

'How do we get back?' Richard said. 'We'll have been seen jumping off by the other passengers.'

'We walk,' James said. 'It's only five miles. We can go to Bluebell Woods.'

'Right, who's up for this?' Daniel said, taking charge for the first time in months.

'It'll be such a lark,' James said.

Richard thought for a moment. He had vowed to keep his nose clean. He had only recently learnt that he had won a scholarship to the grammar school and he didn't want to lose it. But this was just too exciting.

'Okay,' he said.

'Me, me, me!' said George.

'You're not coming,' Danny said brusquely.

'Why not?' said Robert. 'Why is he not coming?'

'Because he's a bloody liability, that's why,' Danny replied.

'He could break his leg when we jump,' James said. 'Or his neck.'

'So could any of us,' Robert said. 'If George can't go, I'm not coming.'

'But...' Danny began.

'Don't bother,' Robert said. 'It's final.'

'Suit yourself,' Daniel said. 'Only I'll not be responsible.'

'No,' Robert said. 'I will.'

In the end, it all went off as planned, apart from a slight hitch at the ticket office. The clerk was a little suspicious, but James had done his homework.

'We're meeting us Mum and Dad off the night train from Glasgow,' he said. 'It gets in at 6.25, I think. Is that right?'

The boys didn't look remotely like brothers but James's attention to detail won the day.

'Aye, lad, that's right,' said the clerk. 'Five of you? That'll be tuppence ha'penny.'

James pushed the money under the metal grille.

'Mind you keep that littl'un away from the platform edge,' the clerk continued. 'And you behave yourselves up there. Think on, now.'

The boys put on angelic faces and touched their forelocks until they were out of sight. Then they scampered up the wide ramp and up the stairs at the far end to the platforms where the tracks ran high above the level of the street.

Once up there, they made their way to Platform 4. Tradesmen were loading goods into the guard's van. They passed through the crowd of workmen and women, and the clerks in bowler hats climbing aboard the third class carriage. The middling sort, professional people, were boarding the second class carriage. None of these paid the slightest attention to the scruffy little band which moved through them towards the panting engine. A man in a morning suit with a top hat was climbing into a first class compartment and a little further on a couple in coats, despite the summer warmth, were also embarking.

Almost all of the first class compartments were empty as James had said they would be. They chose one in the middle of the carriage and pulled the blinds down to deter any other passengers, just in case. Almost as soon as they were aboard, the train began to chug out of the station.

The compartment was luxuriously upholstered. They played with the wall lamps which had frosted glass shades. They admired the framed photographs on each side which featured magnificent buildings. According to their captions, one was of *St Peter's Square, Manchester*, and the other *Manchester Town Hall*. When they thought they must be clear of the station, they raised the blinds again, released the leather straps that lowered the windows and stuck their heads out.

Perhaps the others expected countryside, but James had already discovered that Darwen is just a conurbation of Blackburn and that the route was mostly lined with the backs of mills and factories. The moors reared up on either side beyond them, however, and there were glimpses of Darwen Tower.

Tired of whooping and whistling out of the windows, the boys jumped up and down on the seats and then they put Georgie in the luggage rack and tickled him from underneath.

The journey only took twenty minutes and as the train slowed right down as it approached the shunting yards, James stood by the door. He had to reach right out of the open window to the handle outside.

'Right,' he said. 'When I say 'now', you jump. Rob, you go first, then George, then Rich, then Danny, then me.'

He flung the door open and shouted 'NOW!'

One by one, they jumped and landed safely, apart from Georgie, who curled up like a hedgehog and rolled down an embankment, landing in a ditch. Rob rushed down after him but he was fine and just laughed.

James directed them to a low fence where they could climb over into a quiet street and from there they began their trek back to Blackburn. Just before they reached Lower Darwen, they turned off into a track which led to Sunnyhurst Woods, known as Bluebell Woods to the locals. There they ate their butties watching the widening concentric ripples on the surface of the pond as fish rose to take insects. They saw butterflies in the flowers on the banks and a magnificent dragonfly in the reeds.

Then George played in the little waterfall under the bridge, while Daniel walked into the thick carpet of bluebells in the woods and began picking the flowers. When he had gathered a substantial bunch, James said: 'What are you picking flowers for, you big girl's blouse?'

Danny had been feverishly animated on the train but the sadness had come over him again and he just said: 'I thought I might just pick them for Auntie Elsie for looking after me.' James thought better of continuing his teasing.

They resumed the walk back. The sticky milk from the broken stems had begun to leak onto Danny's wrist and run down his arm and, when he lifted them up, the flowers seemed to have lost their intense colour and to droop. It occurred to him that his aunt would want to know where they'd come from and that he wouldn't be prepared to tell. He let them fall and they lay scattered on the pavement as they walked on.

It was a long walk back to Blackburn and it was late afternoon when they cut across from great Bolton Street to Lower Audley Street. James suggested that they walk the last short stretch along the canal. Daniel just shrugged - he was back in his own dark world again. Rob said he would have to run on ahead. His granny was visiting from Clitheroe and he was expected. Besides, she always had half a crown for him on her rare visits and that wasn't to be sneezed at.

'I'll treat you all if she does,' he said, and ran off.

What followed wouldn't have happened if Rob had been there. He wouldn't have let it happen.

They had barely got down to the towpath when George said: 'Can we stop? I'm tired.'

'We're nearly home, you mardy midget,' James said.

'My feet are killing me,' George said and sat on the ground then and there with his dirty feet sticking out.

He and Richard stood there looking down at him while Daniel walked on a little.

'What's the difference between a river and a canal?' George asked.

'God Almighty!' James said in exasperation.

'Rivers are natural,' Richard said. 'They come down from the hills and flow into the sea.'

'Do canals not go into the sea then?' George said.

'I don't think so,' Richard said.

'What happens?'

'What happens when?'

'When you get to the end? Do they just stop?'

'I don't know. Perhaps they do. Or perhaps they go into other canals.'

'Where do they stop?'

'Perhaps they just do. Like railway tracks.'

'Except you can't have buffers in the water, can you?'

'No, Georgie. Perhaps the water goes into a lake.'

'How does the water get downhill?'

'That's what the locks are for,' Richard said. 'The water is level. The locks let the barges get down to a lower level, that's all. It's like steps made out of water.'

'Richard?' George said. 'You know you said that canals were level?'

'Yeah, they are,' Richard said.

George pointed at the canal.

'Well, why is the water moving?'

'Jesus!' James cried. 'He never stops. Can't you shut him up.'

'Georgie,' Daniel called from further up the tow path. 'come here.'

Daniel had been tinkering with a crane that stood on the canal bank. It was of the kind used for loading barges. The metal tower held a horizontal drum, housing a steel hawser which went up to a pulley which fed another pulley at the end of the jib over which the hawser ran down to an enormous hook with a spherical weight above it. At the other end of the mechanism was a massive counterweight. The whole thing stood on a circular metal plate bolted into the concrete. This was hinged so that the crane could be rotated to pick up goods from the wharf and swing them out to a barge moored alongside. At the moment the crane stood parallel to the canal. The hook had been attached to a metal ring let into the bank but Daniel had managed to unhook it and was moving it up and down using the winch.

The afternoon was very quiet and still. A breeze rippled the surface of the water. The Saturday shift was over and tomorrow was Sunday. There was nobody around.

The other boys came up.

'Do you want a ride, Georgie?' Danny said.

'Yes please, Danny!' George said.

Danny helped George to stand on the hook and the little boy held onto the hawser above him.

Danny winched him up a foot above the ground.

'Higher!' George squealed.

Danny winched him up another foot.

'Higher!'

Another two feet.

'That's enough,' Georgie said. There was a hint of trepidation in his voice. 'I want to come down now.'

'Let him down,' Richard said. 'You can see he's not happy.'

'Give me a hand, James,' Danny said. Together they swung the crane around so that George was now hanging six feet over the water.

'Let me down, Danny. I'm frightened,' George cried.

'That'll learn you not to rabbit on and on,' James said.

'I'll shut up, James, honest I will,' George shouted. 'Cross my heart and hope to die.'

'We're going for our tea now, little Georgie,' Danny said. 'See you later!'

'Bye midget!' James said. 'Enjoy the view.'

He and Danny began walking to the mouth of the tunnel under Audley Range.

Appalled, Richard rushed to the crane and tried to swivel George back to the bank but he couldn't do it on his own.

'Help me, Rich!' George screamed. 'I'm going to fall! I can't swim!'

'Hang on, kid! Just hang on!' Richard shouted.

And he ran after the other two boys, George's screams ringing in his ears. He caught up with them in the tunnel and pinned Danny to the wall by the throat. James was cowed by Richard's rage.

'What the hell are you playing at?' Richard said into Daniel's face. 'You're mad, you are. Now, you come back now and help me get George to the bank or I'll give you a pasting you'll never forget.'

'We were only going to leave him there for a minute,' Danny gasped. 'Let go and I'll come.'

'He was driving us potty,' James said.

'You can just shut up an' all, you evil sod!' Richard said.

When they came out of the tunnel they could see that the lock on the drum had not been engaged properly and had given way. The hawser had run out and the hook had dropped to the canal surface. It had caught in George's jacket and the little boy's body hung just above the canal with his feet in the air and his head under the water.

A pair of ducks came out of the west and landed on the canal further up. So slowly that you could hardly detect the movement, the water slid silently by.

1961 FIRE AND EARTH

THE FACE OF BLACKBURN WAS CHANGING and there was a sense of a new era. They were going to build tower blocks up on Larkhill. They were going to build a shiny new shopping precinct on the old market place. They were going to divert the course of the Blakewater and build a huge covered market between Penny Street and Ainsworth Street, just past St John's Church.

Grown-ups were very exercised about this and most of them seemed to be against it all - the grown-ups we knew anyway. Somebody said that the market hall clock tower was going to be demolished and everybody was outraged and there were petitions and meetings.

We kids were not the least bit interested. None of this had much to do with our timeless world and its routines and rituals.

Besides, Bonfire Night was approaching and there was wood to collect. I have no memory of public bonfires on open spaces - there were no empty spaces in the crowded streets of terrace houses - and certainly no memories of spectacular displays run by public corporations. Bonfires were a local affair, at least in Brookhouse and you bought your fireworks at the paper shop on Whalley Range. The fun lay, not just in the firework display itself, but in lighting your own.

There was a hierarchy of responsibility here. Anything which flew, like rockets or Roman Candles or Aeroplanes, was down to dads and much older boys. This was also true of Catherine Wheels. We were at an age where we were allowed to light colourful but more modest fireworks like: Snowstorms, Volcanoes, Traffic Lights, Golden Rain and Screachers. There were sparklers too for the little'uns like Willie. They were hard to light. Your match could be burning your fingers before the sparkler fired so Mum would light them for us on the gas hob and we would stand in the yard making patterns in the air or trying to write our names with the light traces.

There were also bangers and their deadlier cousins, Flip Flaps, a coil of explosives which would go off in sequence as the firework leapt about. These would make their appearance in school before the big day. They would be dropped over the wall into the girls' playground causing mayhem. Bigger boys let them off on buses or dropped them through the letter boxes of fragile old ladies. We were always up for mischief but this was beyond the pale and we agreed with our parents when they said it was time to bring back the birch, although we were unclear what the birch actually was.

Apart from this, fireworks were confined to just the one day of the year and therefore all the more exciting. Our bonfire was held in the back street. These were cobbled lanes which gave access to the dustbin lorries which would pick up the bins placed at backyard doors and empty them. We shared a back street with Enamel Street and Willie's backyard door was opposite ours. Last year had been really exciting because the backs are relatively narrow and our back door caught fire. There was much hilarity from mothers as our dads tried to put the flames out.

Looking back, I am amazed that these bonfires were ever allowed. I knew that ours wasn't unique - there was another bonfire down the bottom of the backs built by some Catholic kids. I suspect they probably *were* illegal but too common to police. Naturally, we kids couldn't care less.

We looked forward to Bonfire Night intensely. After Christmas it was the most exciting time of the year. The pyramid of wood would be anointed with the old fat from several chip pans and it would flare up as the flames climbed and crackled and fountains of sparks danced into the black sky amid the smoke. There was the coloured glare and dazzle of the fireworks and the distinctive smell of their drifting white smoke with its hints of sulphur and charcoal; the hissing and flaring and banging and the whizz of rockets, the soft detonations as they exploded in the sky; the muted crash and sigh as the pyramid of wood collapsed into the fire and a frenzy of sparks eddied upwards; and there was treacle toffee and baked potatoes.

Mum would always make two trays of toffee: one black, made with treacle, and the other gold with syrup. As the fire sank, the dads would put big potatoes in the embers and have a lovely time turning them with toasting forks or just sticks until they were ready to eat. Then they were fished out and handed round. We would toss them from gloved hand to gloved hand until they'd cooled a little. A few reserved pieces of wood were thrown onto the fire and we would all stand around munching, our backs freezing, our faces flushed, and our eyes wide and watery from staring at the shifting shapes of black, red and gold in the dying embers. And so to bed, dazed with the glamour of it all, rather dirty, full of food, and tired.

'We are going to make this year the best ever,' I said. 'But we need more wood.'

'There was plenty of wood behind St Urban's,' Peter said.

'I'm not going back there again,' Willie cried, tears brimming.

'All right, all right,' said Peter. 'Don't start skriking.'

'Leave him, Peter,' Turdy said. 'You near scared him to death with that stunt down the cellar.'

'I'll bet you were cacking yourself as well,' Peter said nastily.

I suspected that the 'stunt in the cellar' had been an attempt by Peter to regain his leadership. If so, it had failed spectacularly. It had been nearly three months ago and Peter's behaviour since had been prickly and uncooperative. I had the feeling that our little gang was beginning to fall apart. I was at the Grammar now and making new friends and Dennis Flitch's family were talking about emigrating to New Zealand.

'Stop arguing, you two. We're not going back there and that's final. Any road, we don't need to. They've been knocking houses down off Smithies Street. There's bound to be masses of wood.'

'How are we going to get it back here?' Dennis said. 'We can't carry enough to make it worthwhile even if we make several journeys.'

We were standing in the backyard to my house where what we had collected was stacked. It was a good pile but it just had to be bigger than the one further down the back street and so we had some way to go. Today was a Saturday morning. Tomorrow night was Bonfire Night. We needed to get our skates on.

'Well, he's not going to need the pushchair any more, is he?' I pointed to our guy who was sitting lop-sidedly in the pushchair that had been mine as a toddler. He was not very impressive. He was made out of an old bolster. The bottom half was stuffed into a pair of Dad's trousers which didn't fit him any more. Mum said it was because he drank too much beer at the Whalley Range. There was a jacket and shirt that belonged to Turdy's dad and a 'Kiss-Me-Quick' hat that Dennis had bought in Blackpool. He was finished with a clown mask we had bought at the joke shop on the market.

He was a bit of a mess, to be honest, but he'd done his job. We had wheeled him to the doors of the Brookhouse Mill at go-ing-home-time for weeks. As the tides of workers flowed out, we bleated: 'Penny for the guy! Penny for the guy!' as if our lives depended on it. Anyone who gave just a penny got a filthy look, but people were generous on the whole.

We beat the kids lower down the street to this pitch and they had to take their guy along the Bottom to the Star Paper

Mill where the pickings must have been less good because there were far fewer employees. Their guy was miles better than ours but business is business and we established our turf first.

Now, the funny thing was that these kids were from Catholic families.

'Don't you know Guy Fawkes was a Catholic who tried to blow up parliament?' Peter had said to them. 'Why are you burning somebody who was on your side?'

'Yeah, we know all that,' said Patrick Kelly, the leader of their gang. 'It was a long time ago.'

This seemed to me to be a good answer. And to be fair, none of us, Rednecks or Proddy-dogs, thought about history on Bonfire Night.

Turdy said: 'I think Jean's pram is still in the shed.' So we went to look and it was.

Having two vehicles filled us with confidence and we set off down and up the other side of Brookhouse Lane singing 'Ten Green Bottles'.

'Take the dog with you!' Mum shouted from the back door, waving his lead. She never missed a trick, that woman.

'Oh, blurry hell,' I muttered under my breath. 'Go and get him, Willie.'

I kept him on the lead until we had crossed Larkhill. We fell quiet as we passed St Urban's but let Mick go as soon as we reached Primrose Bank.

Now, you'd think an area bounded by Larkhill, Primrose Bank and Mount Pleasant would be idyllic - but it wasn't - it was squalid. The two-up, two-down terraced houses had been empty for ages. And again, you might think that this would have been an ideal playground for us but there were rumours that the whole place was wick with rats and we stayed clear.

I had read in *The Blackburn Times* that the slum was being demolished. As we turned into Smithies Street we could see that the workmen had been busy. Half the street had gone and a start had been made on the other half. A crane with a wrecking ball stood by, and a lorry, covered in dust, was parked near a dying fire which still sent a wavering plume of grey smoke into the cold November air. The raw end of the houses still standing was exposed, fireplaces suspended in the air. Above, slates had slid off the roof and the beams were exposed like ribs.

The cobbles of the street were still intact, running parallel to Mount Pleasant, but the houses on the opposite side were all gone, razed to ground level. A lonely street lamp still stood like a sentry over the chaos. Everywhere there were mounds of broken brick, grey slate, and the terra cotta of chimney pots. There was also wood, masses of it, sticking out of the heaps: great beams which we had no hope of moving, but also shattered planks and spars and staves of wood.

We set to work busily, wearing gloves in case of splinters. I had a leather pair which I had been given for Christmas and of which I was very proud. This would probably ruin them but that didn't matter. This was work of great importance.

My parents had ordered a new wardrobe for their bedroom and Dad had promised that he would smash up the old one for the bonfire if it arrived in time. If we made, say, three journeys from here, I reckoned we could make a Vesuvius of a bonfire that would completely outblaze the pitiful little glow at the bottom of the backs.

When the pram and the pushchair were loaded, we were ready to go and I called Mick. He was busy digging at the other end of the street and didn't stop. I called again but still he didn't come. Much as he loved digging, he was usually obedient and I was puzzled. We went over to see what he was doing.

When we reached him, he was still digging furiously and I had to pull him away by the collar to see what was driving him. There was a large patch of soft, dark earth here and Mick had exposed something white - shockingly white amongst all this dirty debris.

'Here, put his lead on, Turdy, and hold him back,' I said, handing Turdy the lead.

I got down on my knees and started brushing the soil away from the white thing. After a moment or two, it was clear that Mick had found a bone - an animal bone, presumably. I scraped away at it and began to think it looked like a shoulder blade. I knew about this from the St John Ambulance Handbook I had studied at Ben's. Excited, I began to scoop away the soil around it.

Mick was barking like a maniac as the others joined me and it was not long before I exposed what was unmistakably a small human skull.

PART TWO

O keep the dog far hence, that's friend to men,
Or with his nails he'll dig it up again.

T.S. Eliot
The Waste Land

2015   LEAFING BACKWARDS

MY NAME IS TOM CATLOW and I am a retired forensic scientist.
When I was eleven my friends and I discovered a skeleton on a
demolition site. Or rather, my dog did.

It might seem reasonable to suppose that my future career
was determined by that discovery but, as far as I know, there was
no conscious connexion. And, after all, none of my friends went
in for pathology, and nor did the dog. Mick's interest was solely a
question of the eternal canine obsession with bones, though as it
turned out, it had been a very long time since these bones had
had any meat on them.

But I'm getting ahead of myself.

My memory of the event is not particularly strong and it
certainly wasn't traumatic. It would make a very interesting
story, I suppose, if I were to say that the discovery changed me to
the very core and that I bear deep psychological scars, but I
don't. I have a vivid image of the shocking whiteness of bone
against very dark soil and that's about it.

We weren't there when the whole skeleton was unearthed,
you see. We weren't allowed to be. I have a much more vivid image of Mick scampering about, being very pleased with himself
and getting a lot of attention. I loved that dog. When he died -
that was when I first tasted tragedy. He had stopped eating,

couldn't bear to be touched, and had taken to living under the sideboard and could only be coaxed out with great difficulty.

One day, Mum said she would have to take him to the vet and when I came home from school, that was it. He had been put down. Inoperable cancer at the base of his tail. I wept and raged. Mum said that it was kinder this way but all I could say was that it wasn't kinder TO ME and I ran upstairs to hurl myself on my bed in an ecstasy of grief. I hadn't even had a chance to say goodbye.

He did have his moment of glory though when his photograph appeared in both *The Lancashire Evening Telegraph* and *The Blackburn Times*.

This is what happened. We were looking for wood for our bonfire on November 5th, 1961 and we found masses of it where they were demolishing long-empty workman's cottages preparatory to building three tower blocks on Larkhill. As we were loading the old prams we'd brought as transport, Mick found the skeleton. What followed is pretty much a blur. Mike Brown held the dog back while I stood guard with little Willie Melling. Dennis Flitch and Peter Shawcross were sent off to ring the police from the phonebook on Larkhill.

'I haven't got any money,' I remember Peter saying.

We were used to going into phone boxes and ringing 0 for the operator. When she answered (it was invariably a 'she'), we would say: 'Is that the operator on the line?' And when she said 'Yes,' we would say: 'Well, get off it - there's a train coming.'

Dennis said: '999 is free - like the operator. Come on!' And they ran off as if there were some risk that someone would take the glory of the discovery from us or that the body would just get up and walk away.

'It's a skellington, isn't it, Tommy?' Willie said.

'It is,' I said. 'Are you scared?'

'Nah,' Willie said. 'I've seen them before. On the Ghost Train at the Fair.'

Willie had it summed up in a way, I now realise. Our discovery lay somewhere between fact and fiction. Skeletons belonged firmly to the realms of fantasy and I doubt if we made much of a connexion at the time between our find and a once-living human being.

The police were quick. In fact they arrived even before Peter and Dennis came running back. There were three blue and white cars with their sirens going and then there were coppers swarming all over the site. To them, of course, it was a potential crime scene. Radios crackled and dry robotic voices barked and within half an hour another car arrived. A man and a woman got out and foraged in the boot and then got dressed in what looked like baggy white pyjamas. They were, of course, the forensics people, although I didn't know that at the time.

I was keen to see what they were doing but they kept us well away. In fact, we were interviewed one by one, sitting in the back of the police cars. We had little to tell, of course, although I had a great many questions to ask: Was it a murder? Who was it?

When did he die? All they would say was that these were exactly the questions they would be asking but that they would not be able to answer them until they got the body back to the lab and that they might not know even then. Willie asked them if he could have a ride in one of the police cars and could we put some wood in the boot for our bonfire.

One of the most fascinating specialisms within my profession is forensic entomology. This can involve ascertaining how long a body has been dead through insect activity. First to arrive are usually the *Calliphoridae*, attracted by body fluids and gases. These blowflies lay their eggs within a couple of days after death and the development stage - eggs, larvae, pupae, adult - is a useful indicator of how long the cadaver has lain undetected.

Not that this line of enquiry was going to yield any information about our particular corpse.

But I'm getting ahead of myself again. It's like leafing backwards through your memories and turning several pages at a time. My problem is that I'm trying to separate what I now know from what I thought and felt then and it's not easy. The disjunction between someone's experience and their memory of it is very common, as any good detective knows.

What I'm trying to get at is the speed at which the press were on the scene. Throughout my career, I have witnessed their arrival at crime scenes like blowflies at a corpse - swiftly, mysteriously, almost spontaneously. That's what it was like on what remained of Smithies Street on that day when I was a kid, more than half a century ago, though obviously I didn't think of it like that at the time.

The police didn't have much time for the press and gave them the bare minimum of information. They themselves were busy cordoning off the area, lifting the body behind a quickly erected screen, and combing the site for further evidence. We were still hanging about, having given our statements and our 'particulars', even though the cops kept telling us to go home, and so the reporters turned their attention to us. We were willing celebrities.

Not that we had anything to tell them more than we had told the police but our discovery was enough for a front page splash in the *Telegraph*. They took some time about the photograph posing it carefully. In the absence of any substantial information, the photograph *was* the story - for the time being at least.

They had us sitting in a line on a great wooden beam with the black shape of Holy Trinity Church behind us. I was in the middle with Mike and Peter on either side of me and Willie and Dennis at each end. Mick was in front of me. At first, he kept streaking off, and so I had to hold him. The cameraman told us not to smile but to look serious.

'Just hold the bloody dog,' he said.

Even then, every time he said: 'Hold steady now', Mick would look up at me backwards so that all the cameraman could see was the underside of his jaw. He began to get very cross.

At last, Mick obliged. I have the cutting still. As I spread it out on my desk in front me, smoothing out the creases, it is the image of my long-dead dog that moves me, not the poor soul that the police were digging up, just off camera.

There Mick sits with his tongue lolling out of the side of a big grin and, for a moment, the years between then and now seem to vanish. Here is what the newspaper printed in the early edition on November 6th, 1961:

FIVE BOYS AND A DOG DISCOVER BODY

'Foul play cannot be ruled out' - Police
from our Crime Correspondent, Rita Hearne

Five boys from the Brookhouse area made a grim discovery yesterday as they scavenged around a demolition site for wood for their bonfire.

The site is bounded by Mount Pleasant, Primrose Bank and Larkhill and it is being cleared on the orders of the Borough Council to make way for modern high rise flats.

The boys were about to leave the site when Thomas Catlow [11] noticed that his dog was digging furiously in a pile of rubble. When he and his friends went to look, Thomas saw that the dog had unearthed a bone. 'It was quite small and I thought it might be some kind of animal at first,' he told me. 'Then I realised it might be a shoulder bone. I recognised it from a first aid book.'

Thomas, a first year pupil at Queen Elizabeth's Grammar School, Blackburn, continued digging until part of a skull was revealed. 'We thought we'd better ring the police,' he said.

'We can't say very much at this stage,' Detective Sergeant Louis West explained. 'The body has been there for some considerable time and there is very little to go on as yet. We will have more to report once the forensics team have done their work. There may have been an accident but we cannot rule out foul play. Our officers are fine-combing the site for any further evidence.'

Further developments will be reported in due course.

I don't remember a blind thing about the bonfire that night or how - or even whether - we got the wood home safely. No doubt we told our macabre tale with relish and were the talk of the street for a day or two.

The Blackburn Times ran the story on an inside page and there was no photograph so I didn't cut it out. Some sort of vanity may have been at work even then.

Very quickly, I forgot about the whole business. I was loving my first term at school, especially the new subjects.

Dad was very disparaging about Latin. What was the point of learning a language that nobody spoke any more, he would ask. I didn't really have an answer. There was a curious myth current everywhere in my childhood that you needed Latin in order to be a doctor or a lawyer but not otherwise. It ran alongside another myth that all doctors have appalling handwriting.

Well, I'd wanted to be a doctor since I was very small. I could see myself in an unbuttoned white coat with a stethoscope round my neck and pens in my top pocket, like the doctors in *Emergency Ward 10*. When I told Dad about this, he said that perhaps the Latin would come in handy after all. He also said that my handwriting was certainly scruffy enough.

Actually, when I was even younger, I had wanted to be a policeman on Mars. In the end, I suppose I became something part way between a policeman and a doctor, though I had to settle for Worksop and Retford rather than the Red Planet.

2015   MIDDEN

MY FAVOURITE NEW SUBJECTS were the sciences, particularly Biology and Chemistry. We had done some General Science at St John's but this was in a different league. The laboratories were new and well-equipped and the Chemistry labs smelt of gas and sulphur and ammonia and the Biology laboratory had dissected creatures pickled in glass jars and a human skeleton on a stand in the corner. We called him Gerald.

I was doing really well in Biology and was very pleased when my diagram of a bony fish got 9/10 but absolutely elated when my cockroach hit the jackpot and gained full marks. I couldn't wait for the time when I could progress from drawing things to cutting them up.

School helped me both to develop and feed my ravenous curiosity. I had always been obsessed with exploring and questioning. The previous year, my friend Peter and I had explored the course of the Blakewater. To us, it was as exciting as the Amazon or the Limpopo. I had also climbed up the inside of a factory chimney.

Anyway, the Christmas exams were upon us and I was determined to prove myself, especially in my favourite subjects. We sat at our desks in our form room in the Old Huts and scribbled away. The huts had been built as temporary accommodation in the Great War and were still there long after my time. I remember supplementary paraffin heaters had to be brought in to try to combat the draughts. I can still conjure up their stink. When it was all over, the masters came into class and marked the papers and drew up class lists with no pretence whatsoever of attempting to teach us. Our form master, Mr Charnley, said something like: 'I do not care what you do so long as it is not illegal and that there is a modicum of quiet' - so we played battleships and noughts and crosses for two or three days.

When the lists went up I was near the bottom in French and Scripture, in the middle for English, Latin and Physics, but near the top in Maths and Chemistry and top in Biology. And that was it for most of my school life, although my English improved and my Scripture became even worse. It was these aptitudes, I believe, that shaped my future course of study and led me to read Biochemistry at the University of Bristol, where it had begun as a subsidiary in the Chemistry Department and only recently become a course in its own right. I mention this because I believe that school had a bigger influence on my future employment than the discovery at Larkhill.

Now I thought it was just before the Christmas holiday in 1961 that the *Lancashire Evening Telegraph* took up the story again. This time we were only featured in a sentence and it was the skeleton itself that was centre stage. For that reason I didn't keep a cutting. However, I recently looked it up in the Library at Blackburn and the article did not actually appear until January

23rd. The library assistant kindly made a photocopy for me. Here it is:

LARKHILL BODY REMAINS UNIDENTIFIED

<u>Forensic Tests Inconclusive</u>
from our Crime Correspondent, Rita Hearne

Forensic scientists admitted today that they are baffled as to the identity of a body discovered in November by five boys and their dog on a demolition site in the Larkhill area.

Dr Raymond Parker of the forensics unit of the East Lancashire and Ribble Valley Constabulary said: 'All we had to go on was the skeleton. Close analysis of the soil in which the body was found suggests that it was thrown into a privy midden. That means a communal lavatory at the end of a back lane. It would be in an outhouse and would have had to serve several houses.

'Inside there would be a bench with holes in it and the excrement would drop down into the midden. These were foul places and very difficult to clean and so they were gradually phased out towards the end of the Nineteenth Century.'

MISSING FINGERTIP

'All we can say for certain is that the victim was male and six to eight years of age. The nature of the matter in which the body was buried means that bacterial activity stripped the bones of flesh rapidly and completely. There were no identifying characteristics as a result except that the distal phalanx of the third digit of the left hand (tip of the middle finger) was missing. This could have been the result of rodent activity but there were no signs of gnaw marks on other bones so that it was most likely the result of an accident, trapped in a door perhaps.

'Given that there was so little to go on, it has proved impossible to determine the cause or time of death but we are certainly dealing with a historic crime. The body must have been down there for decades. One can only hope that the little boy was already dead before he was thrown into the filth.'

FARTHINGS

'A couple of farthings were found near the body,' Detective Inspector John Ruislip told *The Lancashire Evening Telegraph*. 'Now, they may not have belonged to the victim but they were both from the reign of Queen Victoria. One was dated 1888 and the other 1883. Forensics tell us that it is common for coins to be found where there have been lavatories and indeed other coins were found on the site but none later than 1895.

'The investigation team has ascertained that the houses on Smithies Street, as it was then, had individual outside lavatories built in their yards around 1910, at which point the midden would probably have been sealed off with concrete and the outhouse demolished.

'That suggests that the body was deposited between say 1880 and 1910. It certainly looks as if this was a case of homicide - nobody would throw themselves into such a hell hole voluntarily - though whether we are talking about murder or the disposal of a body after involuntary man-slaughter isn't clear.

'The missing fingertip seemed promising at the time but our missing persons files and medical records at the Royal Infirmary don't go back that far. Dental development is normal for a boy of his age with permanent molars and incisors in place. If the body dates back as far as we think, it was a time when only the rich had access to dentists.'

DEAD END

'The case file remains open though we appear to have reached a dead end. If any member of the public has any information which might be of assistance, I would be delighted to hear from them at the Ainsworth Street station.'

There was much excitement about this at the time. I remember being rather miffed at not being named again and also because they had not honoured the now deceased Mick, as was appropriate to his detecting skills. I made sure it was the talk of the school for a few days and you can bet that we came up with plenty of theories as to how the boy had met his malodorous end. These theories were partly inspired by the film of *Oliver Twist* with Alec Guinness, which had been doing the rounds again. Other theories even involved witchcraft. We lived not far from Pendle Hill after all.

For a while we threatened to murder each other and throw the bodies into the sewers but, before very long, the excitement passed and the rigorous routines of school life took over.

I won't go into much detail about my career path into forensic science, except to say that after Bristol I moved to Cambridge to gain medical qualifications and followed a programme of nine years' study which involved preclinical training, another bachelor's degree, and then clinical training which included a Ph.D. in certain aspects of toxicology. If that's not dedication, I don't know what is. I came out of it with a string of letters after my name and a great deal of hands-on experience. Forensics is a competitive field but my dedication and determination quickly landed me a post with the forensics unit in the Worksop and

Retford Constabulary. After seven years, I moved back to my native county and a post with the East Lancs. and Ribble Valley force. I worked my way up the greasy pole, as it were, and eventually became the Senior Scientific Officer (Forensics) a post which I held until my retirement just over a year ago.

You need a strong stomach for the job. It might seem glamorous on the telly but I can assure you that it is not. There is nothing glamorous about kidney basins of stomach contents; smashed, mangled or even severed limbs; the bloated tissue of victims of drowning; poisoned organs and the various stages of putrefaction, maggots and all. When you see forensic officers at work on the telly, you are spared the smell.

Why do it? Somebody has to. Why does anyone become a proctologist - the medic concerned with the anus and the rectum? Because somebody has to look after the nation's bums. So there's the question of public service. But there's also the question of the chase. There is the burning need to identify the person responsible for the mess on the slab and to bring him (or her) down. People think the word 'forensic' is to do with medicine, but it's not. It has to do with the law. It has the same root as 'forum', the place where justice was dispensed in ancient Rome.

Our workplace is not just the crime scene and the laboratory; we prepare reports for the courts and are quite often called to give evidence - evidence which can convict, or occasionally, acquit. To see justice done, and to know that one has been a significant part of the process, is very satisfying.

I couldn't say how many cadavers have been subject to my scalpel during my long career. I couldn't even begin to count. I will just say that we were always busy, usually with several cases at a time, and that there was therefore no room in my mind for the case of the boy in the midden, or, as we called him at the time: 'the skelly in the bog'.

2015   EVERY MAN SHOULD HAVE A HOBBY

THAT'S WHAT MY WIFE SAID TO ME when I began to contemplate retirement.

'Every man should have a hobby,' she said, 'so what are you going to do? God knows you haven't had any kind of life outside your job for as long as I've known you. I don't want you under my feet all day.'

'That's what my mum used to say.'

'What? You need a hobby?'

'No, I don't want you under my feet all day. Actually, she used to say it about the dog.'

'What's that got to do with anything? Think on now. You need to find something that will get you out of the house. You read about men whose work has been their whole life. They stop work and the next day they drop down stone dead.'

Setting aside Ruth's taste for exaggeration, I knew she had a point. The job had been my everything and she had been incredibly patient with its demands. I was often on call and could be needed urgently day or night. Besides, a certain obsessiveness was a necessity of the job. It gets so that you can't let go until the puzzle is cracked and that can be really stressful. Have you ever gone to bed exhausted after a long journey where you've been driving for hours, and you find you're still driving in your sleep? Well, it's a bit like that.

The Northern Elements

There's the human side too. Of course, you have to distance yourself professionally from what you're handling or you'd go mad. I remember one of our lecturers at Addenbrooke's taking pride in making his students throw up. You have to grow a thick skin and you do it by concentrating on the detail in front of you. That and a measure of black humour.

Just sometimes though, perhaps as you're cleaning up and the porters arrive to take a body off to the morgue, or you're finishing a report for the courts, you suddenly get the whole picture and empathy kicks in. You realise acutely that your subject was once a living being, whose heart beat sixty to a hundred times a minute, day and night, pumping blood around the body, waking or sleeping, until something or somebody stopped the clock. And then what you thought was a carapace that you had grown around you turns out to be soft tissue after all - and you are touched by your own mortality and all the evil and loss in the world.

When I was young and ambitious, I dreaded the idea of retirement but in recent years I came to feel that I have done my duty and that I deserve to be able to sluice down the autopsy table for the last time and to lay down my knives and saws, my forceps and clamps and suturing needles, and to walk out into the clean air.

When it came to it, it was a bit of an anti-climax. I was given a rousing send-off - the police are good at that kind of thing. There was a presentation at the station with speeches and some off-colour jokes. They gave me a bone saw which they'd sprayed gold and had framed, a complete set of Colin Dexter's Morse novels - they must have consulted Ruth - and an impressive watch. There was a 'do' in the evening at the De Tabley Arms near Ribchester, with dinner and dancing, which went on till late.

However, when I got out of bed the next morning, there it was staring me in the face: the future - the rest of my life with no obligations (except to family), no duties, no timetable, no boss, no reports to write, no deadlines to meet, no daily horrors on the stainless steel.

In many ways, I was in a comfortable position. We had moved out to Mellor Brook when I was promoted and the mortgage was paid. The children, who had benefited from an upbringing in the countryside, had left the nest, Nick to Cambridge to read Classics, of all things, and Lisa to York to read Law. Ruth, who had been my rock throughout my career, is ten years younger than me, and is still working as a primary school teacher and loving it.

For the first few days, I pootled along to the Feilden's Arms each lunchtime - because I could. It felt delightfully naughty at first but that soon wore off. The food was excellent, which was a bonus, and the company convivial, and yet, to be honest, it felt like everyone was a bit elderly - though I realise perfectly well that they were no older than me.

Well, that soon palled. I couldn't sit around getting mildly pissed, listening to venerable fogies whining about the changing face of Blackburn, day in, day out until I croaked. I began to wish I'd listened to Ruth and planned my retirement a little better.

It was nice to have time to read but it's a pretty solitary occupation and I needed to be up and doing. One of the fogies took me coarse fishing but - and you'll find this hard to believe given my career - I didn't like handling maggots and bread paste. Besides, I didn't catch a damn thing and felt bored and frustrated. I also tried my hand at golf at Wilpshire Golf Club. I can only say that I am glad I discovered how irredeemably crap I am at the game before I forked out good money on a ludicrously expensive set of clubs. I have always enjoyed walking and tramped along Longridge Fell, or up into the Trough of Bowland, or down to Anglezarke Reservoir. But I'd been used to doing this with Ruth and it wasn't the same on my own. I thought of joining a Ramblers' Association but I felt - almost certainly unjustly - that the image didn't suit me.

During this period of restlessness, the image of the skeleton of a small boy who had died long ago began to insinuate itself into my daydreams. The case had fizzled out according to the press. Now, my temperament is such that I can't do with loose ends. I can't do with fiction, in a novel or in a film, where everything ends up in the air. I know modern authors and *auteurs* (silly word) think it's clever - I just think it's lazy.

Not that forensic science always comes up with the answers like it does on the telly. After a couple of false leads, the detectives always get their man (or woman) and they're often inspired by forensic evidence. I can't give you a meaningful figure for success and error rates on cases, principally solved by reliance on forensic evidence alone. It would vary across the country and much would depend on the kind of case involved. I would guess that it's less than 50%.

Of course, scientific techniques have become ever more sophisticated and the development of DNA profiling has changed the game entirely, making evidence so much more reliable. However, the forensics team can only supply the evidence: it is up to the detectives to interpret it and act upon it. So, back in 1961, without the benefit of more advanced technology, it's not surprising that the agencies drew a blank when it came to our skeleton.

I began musing about this dead end until I felt I just had to go down to the Library and see if I could perhaps spot the shadow of a clue or a missed chance. This is when I asked to see the newspaper entry I've already quoted. I didn't tell Ruth about this. I knew she'd disapprove.

I can't blame Dr Raymond Parker or DI Ruislip for giving up on the case. They had only a skeleton to work on, with next to nothing to identify it or the cause of death. They had done well to put the time of death within some sort of time frame. Now, with the best will in the world, a historic case like this is unlikely to hit the top of the priority list. When attempts to identify the body have failed, when the victim's relatives are long dead and when the perpetrator is beyond justice, you have to ask: what purpose will be served by prolonging the inquiry? - and inevitably, the answer has to be: 'let the dead bury the dead'; there are more pressing cases which affect the living.

And yet, the violent death of a child always tugs at our heartstrings and it is hard to let go. I wondered, just wondered, if long expertise combined with my current leisure might just enable me to take the investigation a little further. I wasn't a detective, of course, but I've worked with the guys long enough to know the methodology.

The itch was upon me. He was my discovery after all, this boy, mine and my dog's.

I was going to reopen the case of 'the skelly in the bog'. I can't keep calling him that. I will call him 'Sam' - that way he's more real - that way, he will matter again, even though more than a century has passed since he perished.

Obviously I was in no position to open this cold case formally and for the moment I was not going to inform my former colleagues. I made the first move by obtaining the photocopy of the newspaper account. My second move would be more difficult. I would have to tell Ruth.

'You are absolutely potty, Tom Catlow,' my wife said when I told her. 'Stark, staring bonkers. You finally get a chance to forget about a job that was making you ill and now you want to take it up as a hobby. Mad as cheese.'

She was beating the hell out of a cake mixture and seemed genuinely angry.

'Who said the job was making me ill?' I said. 'First I've heard of it.'

'Rubbish! What about your high blood pressure?'

'Everyone gets high blood pressure when they're my age,' I said.

'No they don't,' Ruth said. 'What's happened to it since you retired? What did the doctor say when you went for your MOT?'

That's what she calls my annual health review.

'It's come down again, hasn't it?' she said.

'It would probably have come down anyway,' I ventured.

'No it wouldn't,' she said. 'And what about the nightmares?'

'What nightmares?'

'Typical. Every so often you would wake up screaming and frighten me to death.'

'You're having me on.'

'I am not,' she said. 'It's all right for you. You would just say: "Sorry. Bad dream." And you'd turn over and go back to sleep again.'

'Why didn't you tell me?'

'To be honest, I didn't know what to do,' she said. 'I felt sorry for you, I think.'

'You should have said something,' I said, coming up behind her and kissing the back of her neck.

'You used to talk in your sleep as well. Ranting and raving sometimes. Once, you sat bolt upright in bed and shouted: "Please God, somebody stop her. My wife is eating my feet!" Then you fell back on your pillow and started snoring. "Well, thank you very much," I thought. "Is that what you think of me?" I didn't know whether to laugh or cry. All I know is that I didn't get back to sleep that night.'

'But all that probably had nothing to do with the job,' I said.

'Then why has it stopped?'

I had no answer. I had been totally unaware of all this.

'Oh, Tom, can't you let the dead lie? Why do you have to go raking things up again?'

I left her spreading the mixture in a cake tin and went in the sitting room to read the paper. There was a lot of banging about in the kitchen.

Later, I brought her a glass of sherry.

'Ruthie,' I said. 'That little boy was six or eight years old when he died. His body was thrown down a stinking communal privy. He had a mother somewhere. What if something like that had happened to one of the kiddies in your class? What if something like that had happened to our Nicholas?'

That shut her up.

The Northern Elements

2015   MY FIRST INSTINCT

THE WORK OF A DETECTIVE on a murder case is like running a
video backwards. You start with the body and spool backwards:
What does the body tell you? What can you learn about *where* it
was found? *Who* is the victim? *When* did he meet his end? *How*
was he killed? *How* was the body disposed of? - And, at the beginning of the narrative, *why* was he killed?

Of course, in Sam's case, I am working on a presupposition
- that he was murdered. To me, it did seem the most likely con-
jecture. I am inclined to agree with DI Ruislip that suicide must
be out of the question. If you are going to top yourself, there are
sweeter ways to die than hurling yourself into a stinking shitpit.
The canal, for instance? There is the possibility that Sam died of
natural causes, of course, or through some accident and that the
body was subsequently disposed of, possibly by someone who
knew that the broth of bacteria down there in the midden would
strip the flesh off the body in no time. But no, murder seemed
the most obvious possibility.

Then there was the problem of the body. All I had to go on
was a skeleton. I would have to check but it was highly unlikely
that the police would have conserved the remains this long. A
couple of years at most. In the old days an unidentified body
would have been buried in a plot of land called a potter's field, so
called because, in the Bible, the priests bought land as a burial

ground which had previously been owned by potters. In more recent times, the remains would probably have been cremated.

That missing finger tip was interesting, though.

Now, what about the crime scene? Another question arose. Was the scene of discovery the same as the scene of the crime? It is true in general that the kind of hovels which had a common privy would have been breeding grounds for thievery and petty crime, but murder?

Because my recollection of Sam's discovery had been long suppressed, my first instinct was to try to see if my childhood friends had any useful memories of that scavenging morning long ago. Not that I'd stayed in touch with all of them. Dennis Flitch's family had 'flitted' to New Zealand and though I found him on Facebook and sent a friend request, he never replied. Apparently, he's some kind of computer nerd, which doesn't surprise me in the least.

I had better luck finding Mike Brown, who had married a Scots girl and moved to Aberdeen in his twenties. He had worked on the oil rigs in the boom years and had made a packet. He only had patchy memories but he did recall my dog going berserk. He had been charged with looking after the dog while Peter and Dennis had been sent to ring for the police. Mick had been straining on his lead and snarling and even trying to bite Mike when he tried to soothe him. He had had to call me over and we took the dog well away from the site of the skeleton before he calmed down. I'd forgotten this but it came back to me now.

His memory added nothing to the case, but I did take the opportunity to apologise for calling him 'Turdy' for all those years. He said it had never bothered him in the least and that I must pay him a visit to share 'a wee dram or two'. He had obviously gone native.

There was no point in searching for my great friend and rival for power, Peter Shawcross. He had been killed by a drunk driver when he was only nineteen. He had gone to Goldsmith's College in South London and had died instantly when the car mounted the pavement on New Cross Road and smashed into him. His was the first funeral I ever attended. Our relationship had been a little strained at one time and we saw little of each other when we went on to secondary school. All the same, his death touched me deeply and still does, though in a different way.

I have spent my adult life trying to reconstruct narratives where jealousy, greed and revenge have been the most powerful and most common motives for taking the life of another human being, but Peter's death does not - as they say nowadays - compute. A random drunkard loses control of his car just as my friend is - randomly - walking down the same road and reaches the precise point where the curving trajectory of the careering vehicle will destroy him. I don't like this story. It doesn't make sense. I'm sorry, Einstein, God does play dice.

The big surprise was hooking up with little Willie Melling. He still lived in Blackburn, somewhere in Cherry Tree, and though I'd seen him a few times in my teens I'd lost contact. Back then, the epithet 'little' had dramatically ceased to apply. True, he was two years younger than the rest of us but, once he hit his teens, he shot up like a stick of forced rhubarb. By the time, I went off to university he had filled out, and was playing rugby league.

I found him on Facebook pretty quickly and he was up for a reunion. I didn't say why I wanted to see him, because I didn't want to put him off, but he was always a sweet-natured kid. 'For old time's sake' was a good enough reason for him, he said, and we arranged to meet in The Adelphi, one of the few town centre pubs still open.

They say, never go back. Certainly, meeting up with someone you haven't seen for almost half a century can be a bit of a shock. You can't help but be forcibly reminded of your own mortality. With me, it only lasts a few moments: the essential doesn't change - as some writer once said. Willie was bigger, sure, but he still had a good mop of blond hair and had a kind of baby face even at - what? sixty-three he must be - although his complexion was ruddy from an outdoor life. I don't know why I'd ever thought he was an albino. He had dark blue eyes and didn't have to fiddle about with glasses, as I do.

I recognised his gait straight away. I'm good at this. I can tell people I know from a considerable distance by the way they carry themselves. It is almost impossible to define but a person's gait is unique, like their fingerprints or iris. Willie had come in from Cherry Tree by train. I had got to the pub early and though the window was partly frosted, I could pick him out from the small crowd that had spilled out from Blackburn Station with no difficulty at all.

I didn't broach the subject of Sam straight away. I bought Will a beer (I couldn't call this big guy 'Willie') and we set out to fill in the missing years. He had gone from school at fifteen to *The Blackburn Times* and worked his way up from post boy, through cub reporter to Sports Correspondent. I've always hated team games ever since I was a boy and I never looked at the sports pages or I might have seen this. In addition to his column he had done some freelancing for sports magazines and even *The Daily Telegraph* for a spell. More recently, he contributed to *Northern League*, a glossy magazine about rugby league, and then bought it up. He'd done very well for himself and had been able to retire at sixty.

'Have you ever thought,' he said, 'what an amazing time we've lived through? When we were kids the coal - and ice cream - came by horse and cart. You did your shopping down the market. Now, there's under floor heating and if you want something, you go on Amazon and it's there the next day. Incredible.

'When I first started work, we were still using hot metal printing. The typesetters were incredibly skilled. They sat at something like mega-typewriters and the machines automatically slotted the letters into a frame. When the paper had been printed off, the type was melted down in the foundry - the foundry for heaven's sake! - and the letters were cast afresh so the copy would always be crisp - in theory.

'Nowadays, anybody with reasonable software can create a credible newspaper for peanuts.

'But what about you? What have you been up to?'

I told him briefly about my career in forensics. It wasn't a subject I was ever happy to talk about much. There were questions of confidentiality of course, but mostly I didn't wanted to turn the more garish and gruesome aspects of the job into theatre. Even the dead must be allowed some dignity. I did agree with him about the period through which we'd lived and talked a little about the scientific advances which had revolutionised procedures, particularly DNA profiling. I would get around to talking about Sam in due course.

I changed the subject to Ruth and the kids and this was more comfortable ground. I told him how lucky I'd been in finding Ruth and how her cheerful good sense had kept me from the potential nightmares of my work and how, despite the fact that I was often on call, day or night, we had managed to bring up two sane and balanced children. With her help, I had somehow contrived to compartmentalise my work and home life.

Will said he had not been quite so lucky. He had been married for many years, to Marianne, the daughter of a factory owner, but the pressures of journalism had taken their toll. In pursuit of every rugby league match ever played in the north of England, he had neglected his wife. When he began travelling to report on games in South West France, Queensland and New South Wales in Australia, Auckland in New Zealand and even Papua New Guinea, she took a lover - a salesman from Ramsbottom - and their marriage was soon over. He said he had learned to be happy with his own company and that his only regret was having no children.

I refilled our pints and we stared at them reflectively for some time.

Eventually, Will broke the silence.

'Do you ever think about that skeleton we found up Larkhill way, when we were kids?' he said.

'Not for years,' I said. 'Dealing with death every day of your working life, well, it sort of got pushed out of my mind. You?'

'It comes back to me quite often,' he said. 'In fact, I've a bit of a confession to make.'

2015   CONFESSION

HE TOOK AN EXPENSIVE LOOKING WALLET from the inside of his sports jacket and produced from an inner compartment a tiny packet wrapped in tissue paper. He unfolded it and revealed a little silver cross.

'I feel really ashamed about this,' he said with a sheepish smile.

'Go on,' I said.

'I stole it,' he went on. Despite his sixty-three years, he looked like a schoolboy confessing to having half-inched a Mars Bar from a sweet shop.

'Go on,' I said.

'I stole it from the skeleton,' he said. 'I've always felt guilty about it. I felt guilty the moment I picked it up and I always meant to hand it over but the longer it went on, the harder it became. I didn't tell you lot but worst of all I didn't tell the police. And then I thought, I'll get into trouble for not telling them, so I just kept it and shut up. Besides, I was more interested in getting a ride in a police car. I was only eight, remember. I haven't told a soul to this day.'

'So you stole it from Sam?'

'Who?'

'It's what I call him. It seems kinder to give him a name,' I said. 'But where was it, Will? I didn't see any cross.'

'Neither did I, at first, but you had to go and calm the dog down at one point. He was going bananas because you'd stopped him from digging. So I moved in a little closer to... Sam...' (He said the name a little tentatively.) '...and the light must have caught it. It was just next to the skull. I picked it up and shoved it in my pocket.'

'You do realise it might have helped the police to identify him back then?' I said.

'Of course I do,' Will said. 'Why do you think I've felt guilty all these years? Do you remember when Peter played that trick on us in the cellars at the back of the Catholic church?'

'I do now,' I said.

'Well, somehow, I thought that the cross would protect me from evil spirits. Oh, I knew perfectly well that Peter had faked the apparitions that afternoon but you don't think that logically at eight, do you?'

'I suppose not,' I said. 'Let me have a look at that cross. Is it real silver?'

'Oh yes,' Will said. 'I had it checked. There's a hallmark on the back. It might even be valuable. It's quite old.'

'Would you mind if I borrowed it?' I said. 'I promise the bogies won't get you.'

Will laughed.

'Sure, but why? I thought you said you'd forgotten about "Sam".'

Now seemed to be the time to explain my retirement plan to try to resolve Sam's case. Will seemed intrigued from the start.

'It's ironic, isn't it, that all through my working life, Ruth complained about my being called away so often, and now she can't wait to kick me out of the house? I think I've pushed this business down into my subconscious and it's time to lay it to rest. If I were religious, I'd be talking about laying the boy's troubled spirit to rest too.'

There was a long pause.

'I could help you, if you like?' Will said.

'You?'

'Oh, I know I haven't got your scientific expertise but I might be some help with the press archives, for instance.'

'I'm sorry, Will,' I said. 'I didn't mean to be patronising. That would be great. You could make some appeasement to the boy's spirit for stealing his cross.'

'If I were religious.'

'If you were religious.'

'How do you know the skeleton was a boy's, by the way?'

'Ah, my turn to produce some evidence,' I said and I took out my own wallet and produced the photocopy of the newspaper report I had obtained from the Library. Will read it carefully a couple of times and gave me a rueful look.

'Not much to go on, is there?' he said.

'Afraid not,' was all I could say.

'Let's see what we've got then,' and from another pocket, he produced a ballpoint pen and a small black reporter's notebook, secured with a black elastic band. He saw me grinning and grinned back.

'Old habits,' he said and started making bullet points which he read out as he wrote.

- *Male*
- *6-8 years old*
- *Skeleton found in privy midden*
- *Disturbed by demolition work November 1961*
- *Missing fingertip, third finger, left hand*
- *Farthings found near body*
- *Suggest disposal between 1880 and 1910*
- *Homicide likely*
- *Silver cross found near skull*

'I like it, Watson,' I said.

'What?'

'This systematic approach.'

'Patronising git,' Will said.

'One thing doesn't seem right. It's been niggling me. That bit about dentition seems to suggest that Sam was from a poor background. But that's not necessarily the case, is it?'

'How do you mean?' Will said.

'Well, there seems to be an underlying assumption that the boy was poor. That's why the police didn't go looking for dental records. But it doesn't necessarily follow that the victim was poor just because he was found in a deprived area. And now there's a silver cross. What would a pauper be doing with a silver cross?'

'Unless he was a Roman Catholic,' Will said.

'Oh, you're good, you are,' I said.

'He was found just around the corner from St Urban's. That was a Catholic area when we were kids. There's no reason to suppose it was any different in Victorian times. There might just be something in the church records.'

'If we knew what we were looking for,' I said.

'True,' Will said ruefully, 'though I reckon he must have been killed nearby. What would be the point of trekking around town with the body of a dead child?'

'Oh, you'd be surprised the lengths people will go to dispose of a body. The first thing we need is the child's identity.'

'So what's the plan?'

'OK. I am going to get permission to find out what happened to the body. I think it is most likely that it was cremated but you never know. Christ knows the poor creature can't have occupied much space. Even if the body was disposed of, there may be something in the records which might help.

'Meanwhile, do you think you could take a look at the newspapers?'

'I thought you'd done that,' Will said.

'For 1961, yes,' I said. 'No, I mean the Victorian ones - and the Edwardian ones. It's a tall order, I know.'

'Thirty years. It might take as long as that before I find anything material, of course, but I'll give it a go.'

'I should start somewhere in the middle, if I were you, and work outwards,' I said.

'The voice of experience.'

'Exactly.'

'I'll look in *The Blackburn Times* archives, though I don't think it was called that then, and I'm fairly sure *The Lancashire Evening Telegraph* had another name as well. I'll see what the Library has got, if anything. I'll also pop over to Preston and see what the County Archive can come up with.'

'You'll make a fine detective one day, Watson,' I said.

'Why, thank you, Holmes,' Will replied.

'We shall call it *The Case of the Boy with the Missing Fingertip and the Silver Cross*,' I said. 'Your round, I believe.'

Relieved that we had a plan, touched by Will's confession, and relaxed by the beer, I forgot my former reticence about my past career and began to tell him about *The Case of the Decomposed Body in the Trawl Net* at Fleetwood, T*he Case of the Man Accidentally Hanged by his own Jacket* in an orchard near Grange-over-Sands, *The Strange Death of a Soldier* who died from 'swallowing large masses of unmasticated food' in a pork pie eating competition in Lancaster, and *The Case of the Man who Set Fire to his Wife* in Padiham.

2015   BLIND ALLEYS

POLICE WORK, and more specifically, forensics, is a slow, painstaking business carried out under intense pressure to produce quick results. One learns not to succumb to pestering or duress though it is always there. Everything must be sifted and analysed and assigned to its proper place and time in a chain of events.

There is no template because every case is different. There are routines, of course, but they do not always take you where you expect. Sometimes, in fact, you learn as much by what is not found than what is. There is the imprint of a wristwatch on the skin but no watch. Why? The left sock is missing despite the fact that the body is wearing both shoes. Why? You have to learn to ask the right questions.

I had not expected Sam's case to be quite so difficult. I had no problem accessing the records of the case - my former boss was happy to let me pursue a bona fide inquiry though he did say that he thought I was probably on a fool's errand. The records had been written up meticulously by DI Ruislip although, as I had expected, the body had been stored for two years and then cremated. There were photographs, however. Dr Parker, the forensics man, had taken several from different angles and there were a number of close-ups. Any faint hopes I might have had of interviewing either of these two gentlemen were quickly dashed. Both had died before the Millennium.

I studied the photographs with great care but they told me little we didn't already know. It was frustrating. With modern biochemical techniques I could have learnt so much from those poor bones. I could see the absence of the finger tip and distortion to the phalanx below it, but it didn't tell me much. The dentition suggested that the estimated age of the boy was correct, though I was more inclined to say that he was nearer eight than six.

In fact, though the reports seemed to take it for granted that the body was that of a boy, I couldn't see how they had determined that from the skeleton alone. Differences in the development of the pelvis and the skull only come with puberty. This could have been the skeleton of a girl. I was beginning to feel that I knew less now than when I started. It was as well that I'd given our victim the name Sam which was not gender marked.

Nor was I any clearer about Sam's social class. There was no evidence of serious malnutrition such as incipient rickets, a skeletal disorder caused by lack of vitamin D or calcium. That in itself told me very little. The poor might very often go hungry for a time but when they did eat, their diet could sometimes be healthier than that of modern kids raised on burgers, doughnuts and cola.

The farthings found near the body I was inclined to discount as being of little importance. They may not even have belonged to Sam and offered only a very circumstantial time frame for the disposal of the body - and thirty years was a very big window, as Will was no doubt finding.

The thought prompted me to ring him with the disconcerting news that we couldn't be sure of the gender of the child and to apologise for not having thought of that earlier.

'Well, it makes little odds,' he said. 'I don't seem to be making much progress either. I've started with *The Blackburn Evening Standard and Weekly Express* in 1890 and I've been leafing backwards, as it were. This is going to be a long job. I haven't quite got through a year's papers yet.'

'It's not as if we're in a hurry, is it?' I said.

'No, but we're not immortal either, are we?'

'Where are you working?'

'I'm at home at the moment but I've been working in the Library. They've been incredibly helpful and given me access to the British Newspaper Archive. It's eye-straining work and the archive isn't complete. We may have to think of a trip to the British Library, if I don't find anything. I do have a couple of bits and pieces - generic stuff - not about our Sam, but - well, you might find them interesting.'

'Why don't we meet up at The Grapes on Friday lunchtime?' I said. 'It's near the Library and we can compare notes. If it's too depressing we can at least get a decent pint of Thwaites.'

Will thought it a good idea and we duly met up and ordered pies and pints.

'Thing is,' Will resumed, 'there's not a great deal about missing kids at all, and when there is, it's tucked into a corner. It's not like nowadays where photographs are plastered all over the papers, on the telly and through social media. People share the images whether they knew the kid or not. I feel uncomfortable saying it but it helps if the kid is good-looking.'

'And if the parents have the means to promote the search,' I said.

'Definitely that. Look at this.'

Will took an A4 photocopy out of a document case and smoothed it out. It featured a couple of columns of densely printed classified advertisements, in very black ink and a messy variety of fonts. He had ringed one advertisement with a felt pen. It read: 'Dr. & Mrs. Geo. Fletcher-Hawes, of "The Cedars", Shear Bank Road, Blackburn, are delighted to report the safe return home of their son, Timothy, missing for two days. They wish it to be known that they are much beholden to their friends and members of the public for their fruitful intelligence, and their solicitude and counsel.'

'Was there an antecedent?' I asked. 'I mean, did they place an ad earlier to report him missing?'

'If they did, I can't find it.'

'Posh address.'

'Certainly is. There's that and his title and the double-barrelled name,' Will said.

'And the educated vocabulary,' I added.

'And the length of the insert,' Will said. 'That would have cost a pretty penny.'

'Why do you think there wasn't an earlier ad?' I said.

'Well, we're definitely dealing with someone from the middle classes - upper middle probably. My guess is that people of that sort would feel a kind of shame at having their child go missing - as if, you know, they feared that people might accuse them of neglect.'

'Whereas, they would be only too happy to go public when the lad was found safely? I see what you mean.'

'Besides,' Will said, 'I reckon these people must have had enough money to lean on the authorities to do everything possible to find the boy.'

'So where are we?' I said.

'I just don't know,' Will said. 'I've found three or four accounts of the *bodies* of missing children being found but no reports of them going missing in the first place. Why do you think that is?'

'Children go missing all the time,' I said. 'Most of the time they're found within twenty-four hours. Did you ever run away as a kid?'

Will laughed.

'Didn't everybody? I only got as far as Bastwell,' he said.

'And I'll bet you were back by teatime?'

He nodded.

'There you are,' I said. 'Most missing kids turn up miraculously as soon as they're hungry.'

'So you're saying they're only news if they're dead?'

'It's a theory,' I said, without much conviction.

'Well, I'll tell thee summat,' Will said. 'This sleuthing business is doing my eyeballs in. Imagine pages and pages like this.'

He pointed to the photocopy.

'The front page is all adverts: adverts for gout pills; arthritis pills; whooping cough pills; pills for housemaid's knee and tennis elbow; adverts for funeral arrangements; milliners; gentlemen's outfitters of discretion and discernment; stables and smithies; excursions to Blackpool and Southport, the Lakes and even Paris; adverts for public lectures and public meetings and trusses. Everywhere there are advertisements for trusses.

'On page two, there is usually a long short story and a column in Lancashire dialect which I have to confess to finding pretty opaque, even for a lad born on "Animal" Street in the middle of the last century. And then there are more adverts - for farmers and farriers, and even more pills and potions, and ladies' hats. And trusses. More trusses. You'd think Lancashire had a monopoly on hernias.

'There are no photos to break this thicket of type up, Tommy, just the occasional sketch - of a lady's hat - or a truss. And, you know what? What we would call news nowadays is

175

buried amongst all this, with no banner headlines or increase in font size to identify it. And I tell you, after a couple of hours of working through this, your eyeballs are on fire and you look up and the world is a blur.'

'So what are you saying?' I said. 'Do you want to give up?'

'Give up?' Will said. 'Do I 'eck as like want to give up.'

2015   FIVE BOYS

WHEN WILL AND PETER and Dennis and Turdy Brown and I were lads, there was a chocolate bar called Fry's 'Five Boys'. I have since learned that the brand was launched in 1902 and I'm not surprised that it goes back that far. The wrapper seemed weirdly old-fashioned even in the early sixties and that was part of its attraction. That and the fact that there were five portions to a bar which made it very convenient for sharing.

At first glance there appeared to be five boys on the front of the wrapper but, if you looked closely, it was the same little boy, in an Edwardian sailor suit, photographed in medium close-up so as to exhibit five different emotions with regard to the prospect of the chocolate within. In order, the little chap was expressing: desperation, pacification, expectation, acclamation and realisation ('It's Fry's'). Pretty ponderous, I know, and the forensic scientist in me suggests that the stimulus for the image was probably Charles Darwin's remarkable, but sometimes misguided book, *The Expression of the Emotions in Man and Animals* (1872). But hey, that's not the point. Ponderous or not the images lasted until 1976, when Cadbury's, who now owned the brand, sought to modernise the product and replaced the now iconic photographs with cartoons. The product bombed and was never seen again.

I mention it because it came straight to mind when Will made our first substantial breakthrough. It reminded me that, at the time, Fry's Five Boys Chocolate seemed to me to symbolise our gang. It sounds daft, I know, and it's true that there was only one boy, but there were five emotions. Through some kind of submerged nexus of association in my mind, the unity of the group - despite the diversity of our feelings - seemed to be invested in the image on the wrapper. This wasn't conscious, of course, and I'm only beginning to rationalise it now.

Will's news was about another five boys, another little gang, much like ours in many ways, who had lived and played in the streets of Blackburn seventy years before us. And that's what brought the images on the chocolate wrapper to the forefront of my mind.

I'm rambling again and getting ahead of myself, which isn't good, because I want to keep things in order and I should know better.

After our meeting in The Grapes, Will and I decided we would meet weekly whether we had anything to report or not. Ruth approved of this. She had come round to thinking of our search for Sam's history as more like a hobby after all and she certainly gave her blessing to my renewed friendship with Will. I had told her about his divorce and she was sympathetic.

'So much better than you mooching down to the Fielden's or stagnating about the house,' she said. 'Why don't you bring him home for dinner some time? It's half term soon.'

'Certainly not,' I said. 'You'll only try to mother him.'

In order to change the subject, I showed her the little silver cross I'd borrowed from Will.

'Oh, Tom, it's beautiful!' she said. 'When you mentioned it, I imagined it would be something cheap and simple. Do you remember that Catholic stall on the market when we were kids, the one that sold rosaries and plastic figures of the Virgin and little bottles for holy water? I bought a little silver cross with my pocket money - actually, it was probably stainless steel or something. My mother thought I was going through a religious phase because I bought a crucifix to hang on the wall as well - but the little cross was for cosmetic reasons and the crucifix was for a story I planned to write. The body of Jesus glowed in the dark, you see. A kind of lurid green.'

'But this is in a different league, Tom. It's beautiful! Look at this filigree work. So delicate.'

'I'm going to see what Eric Aspinall thinks of it,' I said. I'd worked with Eric in Forensics for many years. He was an expert in jewellery.

'Oh, can't I keep it?' Ruth said.

'No, you bloody can't,' I replied.

Eric was intrigued.

'Yes, it's silver all right,' he said. 'Where did you get this?'

I told him as much of Sam's story as he needed to know, without revealing Will's guilty secret.

'All right,' he said, handing me his jeweller's eyepiece. 'Take a look at the hallmark. What do you see?'

'It's quite worn,' I said. 'It looks like some sort of bird and there's a letter D.'

'Correct,' Eric said. 'That there bird is a cock, which tells me that your cross is French, made in Paris by Maurice Duguay in the 1790's.'

'So, Sam was from a wealthy Catholic French family?' I said.

'Whoa. Not so fast,' Eric said. 'You know better than that. It may be quite valuable now because of its age but the silver is not particularly high calibre and old Maurice could have been knocking these out pretty fast. Catholic? Probably. French? Somewhere along the line. Perhaps a couple of generations back. Who knows. My guess is that it's an heirloom, passed down through the family. I'm afraid it doesn't tell us anything conclusive about the class or financial status of the boy.'

Seeing my obvious disappointment, he decided to rub it in, as was his wont.

'Of course, you can't rule out the very real possibility that the boy stole it.'

'You are a little ray of sunshine, Eric,' I said. 'You know that, don't you?'

'Was there a chain?' he asked.

'No mention in the record,' I said. 'And no sign in the photograph.'

'Now, I don't know about you but I think that fact alone is very suggestive?'

'Got you,' I said. 'It's understandable that the cross might have become detached but it was very close to the neck which suggests he was wearing it. Now, if it had been attached to a chain, that would still have been around the corpse's neck. We must be looking at something biodegradable. String, perhaps?'

'Or a length of ribbon?' Eric said.

'Ribbon, yes, I like it,' I said, 'which suggests a relatively poor background and a treasured heirloom. And, and, and…'

'And what?

'And this: it was treasured, not found or stolen, because if it had been, it would have been rushed round to the nearest pawn shop and turned into ready money.'

'Bingo,' Eric said. 'Do you want your old job back?'

'Nah,' I said. 'I much prefer this amateur stuff. A man should have a hobby, you know.'

I walked into The Grapes that Friday feeling like the cat that got the cream.

'Breakthrough time, Will,' I said with the smug air of a TV quiz presenter.

'I've got something too,' Will said.

'Go on then,' I said, taking a swig at my beer.

'No, you first,' Will said. 'You've got foam on your lip, by the way.'

I wiped it off and told him about my discussion with Eric.

'You didn't tell him I'd trousered the cross, did you?' he said.
'Of course I didn't,' I said. 'What do you take me for?' I
handed it back to him in a little evidence sachet supplied by Eric.

'I think I've got a couple of leads too,' Will said modestly.
'And what's more. I think we have a tie-in. Here, give this a sken.'

He took a photocopied sheet from his document case and
pushed it towards me. This time it was lengthier and much more
detailed. It was Will's turn to look smug. His lead trumped mine
by an order of magnitude. It was from *The Blackburn Standard*
of Saturday, August 29, 1891 and it read:

AT BLACKBURN MAGISTRATES COURT, on Monday last (Arthur F. Hindle, JP, presiding) Mrs Marie-Pierre Pickford,
of Withers Street, Blackburn, was fined the sum of one
penny for causing an affray and bound over to keep the
peace in the sum of one shilling and threepence.

Sgt. P. Beardsworth of the East Lancashire Constabulary deposed that the said Mrs Pickford, in extreme dis-
tress because her son, George, had gone missing two days
previous, had made a continuing public nuisance of herself outside the Ainsworth Street police station.

It appears that her son, George, had not come in from
play on the afternoon of Saturday, August 22nd, and nor
had he been seen since. She had reported the child's disappearance on the Saturday evening and had at first refused to leave the police station.

When she was put outside she began a lamentation in the street so ostentatious and unseemly as to be alarming to passers-by. She also commenced to protest most vocally that the police were not doing enough to find her son. She kept up these ululations through Saturday night and into Sunday, until she was arrested at four o'clock in the afternoon.

Her husband, Terence Pickford, mule spinner, of the River Street Mill, apologised to the Court for his wife's behaviour and said that he had tried in vain to get her to return home with him.

Sgt. Beardsworth deposed that, contrary to the woman's protestations, the police were doing everything within their powers to trace the missing child. Officers had interviewed the last known persons to have seen the child, these being his habitual friends, namely: Richard Clayton of Higher Audley Street, Daniel Catlow of Maudsley Street, and James Bibby of Ingham Street.

The boys had testified that they had been together all day but had separated on the canal towpath at the bottom of Bennington Street. Robert Harrington of Scotland Road had been with them earlier but had gone home and could add nothing.

Sgt. Beardsworth told the court that the area had been cordoned off and that police divers were on the scene.

Concluding, Mr Hindle addressed the defendant thus:

'Madam, it is because I recognise the legitimate intensity of your grief that I have been minded to impose on you a merely nominal penalty. I pray to Almighty God that your son be found soon and in good health and so do we all.

'However, I must tell you that any interference with the police as they go about their proper duties is not to be tolerated. I therefore bid you: go home and watch and pray, but mind you keep the Queen's peace. Mr Pickford, sir, I charge you keep your wife at home and give her protection and solace, as is your marital duty.'

If any reader of this periodical has any information whatsoever regarding the disappearance of George Pickford, aged 8, they should inform any police officer or the offices of *The Blackburn Standard and Weekly Express* forthwith. The boy is 3 feet, 10 inches tall. He is fair-haired and the tip of the middle finger of his left hand is missing.

Five boys!
The missing fingertip.
And my own surname leapt off the page at me.

2015   ANOTHER BRICK WALL

'DON'T YOU THINK it's kind of ironic,' I said, 'that you come up with the goods, when I'm the one with the training in forensic science?'

'Hey, I didn't realise it was a competition,' Will said with a grin.

'Of course, it isn't,' I said, though, if I'm really honest, I have to admit to being slightly miffed that I had come up with next to nothing while an ex-sports correspondent had made a significant breakthrough. Perhaps part of me still saw Will as the little blond urchin who could be ordered about.

'All I've managed to come up with is the provenance of the silver cross,' I said. 'And that gets us precisely nowhere.'

'Ah, but don't you see?' Will said. 'That's the tie-in.'

'How come?'

'Sammy's mother. I mean George's mother. Her name? "Marie-Pierre" is hardly a Lancashire name, is it?'

'God, you're right, aren't you?' I said. 'Hyphenating a female name with a saint's name is definitely French.'

'So perhaps George's family *were* catholics?' Will said. 'The cross would have been handed down.'

'Hang on though,' I said. 'These addresses are all in the Audley area. That's protestant territory. These boys would have gone to St Martin's, or Holy Trinity at a pinch. My hunch is that George had a catholic mother and a protestant father.'

'And a child from a "mixed marriage" wouldn't have been welcome at St Urban's in those days,' I said. 'It was still the case when we were kids. The marriage would only be recognised if you promised to bring up any kids as Catholics. I'm guessing the father - what was he called? - Terence, wasn't having it. I just feel it in my water that those boys went to the same school. This is all speculation, of course.'

'I don't suppose there are records of school rolls back then?' Will said.

'No,' I said. 'Digital registers hadn't been thought of in the 1880's. Didn't you know that?'

Will curled his lip at me.'

'I'll tell you what though,' I said. 'You could check the baptismal records at St Urban's and St Martin's. Then there's the register of Births, Marriages and Deaths at the Town Hall.'

'I'm not sure where all this is getting us,' Will said.

'Maybe nowhere,' I said, 'but we want to try to build a profile for these lads. They say they left George by the canal. Did he fall in? The body at Larkhill was definitely his. We know that from the cross and the missing fingertip. So how did it get there? My guess is that the other boys must have known something they didn't tell the police. I'm sure of it. Why did George go off in a different direction?'

'And why do you think Marie-Pierre didn't mention the cross to the police?' Will said. 'As a means of identification, I mean.'

'Good question,' I said. 'If my hunch is right, maybe she practised her Catholicism in private. Maybe George's dad didn't even know the lad had the cross and maybe she didn't want him to know. Maybe it was a little secret between Marie and her little boy.'

'A lot of *maybe's* in that, Tom.'

'That's how it works, mate. You come up with hypotheses and you test them to destruction.'

'So where do we go from here?' Will asked.

'I don't feel I should be giving orders when you made the big break through,' I said.

'Never mind that,' Will said. 'What do you want me to do?'

'Well, you can carry on with the paper trail, if you will. See if there's any follow up on that report. And check the baptismal records and also hatches, matches and despatches.'

'Eh?'

'Births, Marriages and Deaths,' I said. 'Keep up, son.'

'Ah, right,' Will said. 'And what are you going to do?'

'I have a little plan of my own which I don't want to tell you about because it will probably come to nothing and I can't have you laughing at me, can I?'

'As if I would...' said Will.

'Yeah, as if...' I said, laughing.

Shortly after I retired, and while Ruth's nagging at me to find a hobby was at its most insistent, I sent away for a DNA testing kit to one of those genealogy sites. I don't know what I was expecting exactly. I probably hoped, like most people who take up genealogy, to find that one of my ancestors was a royal duke, or better still, a highwayman, or even one of the signatories to the death warrant of Charles the First. Rather childish really.

Anyway, the kit duly arrived. It involved a saliva collection tube and a pre-paid envelope to send it off to their lab along with instructions on how to register on the site. I would receive an email in a couple of weeks. Of course, I could have printed out my DNA profile at the forensics lab anytime I wanted but I would only be able to link it to the police database. This site promised the possibility of links across the world - and not only to suspected felons but law-abiding citizens too. I followed the instructions, hoping that Booth's Assam tea and fragments of Jaffa Cake might not contaminate the sample.

I became quite excited as I waited for the result and Ruth commented wryly that I'd never properly grown up. She had a point, I suppose. This was like waiting for my *Beano* membership pack, with a badge and a certificate when I was eight or something.

The result was a considerable disappointment and told me nothing I couldn't have guessed already. There was an ethnicity estimate that suggested 78% of my ancestry could be focused on

The Northern Elements

Northern England; 17% from County Galway in Ireland; 3% from the Iberian Peninsula and 2% from Western Europe. The Iberian bit meant nothing to me: sixteenth century corsairs? Portuguese explorers? As for Western Europe: a bit of hanky-panky in any one of many European wars through the centuries? There was a kind of Venn diagram laid over a map of Europe and the area of maximum concentration was Lancashire.

Well, big deal. I'd paid over ninety quid for this. I just thought it was fairly obvious that people of our class would stay put for generations, especially where there was work to be had, which was still true in my early childhood. The final terminal decline of the cotton industry would come throughout my lifetime.

There was a tab which said 'Build Your Family Tree' and I tapped it. It suggested that if you filled in what you knew, with dates wherever possible, the site would look for matches and that any other data from other family members on the site might help the tree to grow. I had little information to fill in. My father, David, died in 2005 and my mother, Lucy (née Croasdale) in 2010.

It is only when both your parents are dead that you realise there are so many questions you want to ask them and that it's too late. What else could I add from my own memory?

I knew that my paternal grandfather was called Thomas and that I had been named after him. He lived two doors up from us on Brookhouse Lane. He died when I was only five and I

189

have only the vaguest memories of him as a very old man, though he was only forty-five at his death. Dad said that cancer had drained the life out of him and bent his back.

He had an older sister called Cassandra who lived until 1990, dying at the grand old age of 92. She never married. I remembered Great Aunt Cassie because of her annual Christmas present. She would arrive in great state a week before Christmas wearing a hat, even indoors. The present was always the same: a ten shilling note folded tightly and slipped into a little envelope which she had made herself out of coloured paper. Ten shillings was quite a treasure to a small boy in those days.

When the 50p coin replaced the ten bob note - in 1969, I think it was - I would receive 50p in a little envelope just the same. I was at university then and I remember it was enough to buy three pints of beer. She carried on giving me 50p, making no adjustment for inflation, until she died, when I was 40 and the little gift had become something of a family joke. That probably sounds a bit callous, but to be fair, I hardly knew her. She lived in Bastwell on Ash Street. I think my mother used to visit her from time to time.

Well, I filled all this in and expected nothing from it. I had more or less decided that my membership fee had been a waste of money and that genealogy was not going to be the hobby for me. In fact, I forgot about it until Will and I were talking about baptismal registers and so on. When I got home later that Friday, I checked the site for the first time in over a year. On the map, the Iberian connexion had disappeared and the Irish one increased by 2%. I found that strangely pleasing. Better still, a distant cousin several times removed (no, I never understood that stuff either) had populated many parts of the tree including my branch of the family. She was called Arianna Slater and was now living in Canada.

My eye went straight to one name. Daniel Catlow was the father of my Great Aunt Cassandra and my grandfather, Thomas. He was born on July 1st, 1880 and died on his 36th birthday in 1916.

George's friend, Daniel, was my great grandfather.

I couldn't wait to tell Will and when we met at The Grapes the following Friday we were both buzzing.

'What have you got?' I asked.

'You first,' Will said.

'No, you,' I insisted. I wanted to hold out on the drama of my discovery as long as possible, I suppose. Perhaps, I wanted to be the one to trump Will this time.

'Right,' he said. 'I couldn't find any follow-up to the missing boy story in either *The Standard* or *The Blackburn Times*.

'But - baptismal registers. Nothing at St Urban's. It seems all five boys were christened at St Martin's and probably went to St Martin's School, which bears out your theory that if Marie-Pierre was a French Catholic, her religion was overruled by her husband.'

I licked the tip of my forefinger and described a large tick in the air.

'The only relevant death certificate I could find,' Will continued, 'was for Robert Harrington, who became a policeman and died in 1940 aged sixty. If he knew anything about what happened to George, he took it to his grave. Mind you, he wasn't with the others when they left George. So that figures.'

'Marriage certificates?'

'Nothing. Though traditionally marriages take place in the bride's church, of course. I did find this though.'

He passed me another photocopy of a page from *The Standard* of January 15th, 1898, where he'd ringed an entry under 'Announcements'. It read:

> MR AND MRS FRANK CLAYTON wish to congratulate their son, Richard, on gaining a place at Trinity Hall, Cambridge, to read law. They would like to thank the masters at QEGS, Blackburn and his teachers at St Martin's School for their part in his education.

'Local boy makes good, eh?' I said.

'Exactly,' Will said. 'Probably moved out of Blackburn when he qualified, taking his secret with him. Too posh for the likes of us. Anyway, what have you found?'

I told Will about my family tree and how Daniel Catlow was my great grandfather. I showed him a printout.

'That's incredible,' Will said. 'And look, he died on his birthday. Only 36, poor sod. Hang on a minute. July 1st, 1916. Wasn't that the first day of the Battle of the Somme?'

'Do you think he copped it then? It was a wipe-out, wasn't it, if history lessons serve?' I said.

'They're bound to have records of those who fell in the Great War at the Library,' Will said, 'You could check it out. Mind you, it isn't getting us anywhere. I mean, it's all fascinating and all that but it isn't getting us any nearer to what happened to George and why he was dumped where he was. It's just a brick wall.'

'True. Another brick wall,' I sighed.

2015   GREAT AUNT CASSIE'S LEGACY

OFTEN YOU FIND SOMETHING when you've stopped looking for it. Once, I lost my specs. I turned the house upside down and searched high and low for them. Only when I'd bought a new pair, at considerable expense, did I find them - at the back of the fridge. How they got there, I still don't know. Or rather, I know that I put them there, but *why* I can't imagine. I can only suppose that I'd come home from work absolutely exhausted, as was often the case, and in a pre-bed stupor gone to the fridge for a snack, taken them off and left them on a shelf.

On another occasion I mislaid my keys at work. They were quite a big bunch and had worn a hole in more than one pair of trousers. Fortunately, my car keys were in my overcoat and Ruth would be in when I got back, but it was a nuisance nonetheless. There was an emergency set of house keys at home, so that was not a problem, but there had been one or two work keys on the ring, including one that gave access to certain reserved chemicals. It was an embarrassment, to say the least.

Of course, I'd gone around the place asking everyone if they'd seen them and I'd had to grit my teeth when people said: 'Where did you see them last?' I know people mean well but, if you think about it, it's a pretty stupid response, isn't it? I mean, if I knew where I'd last seen them, they wouldn't be lost, would they?

Anyway, that night I dreamt that they were on my desk at work underneath a heap of dark blue folders which I'd lain on top of them. When I'd searched my desktop and moved the folders about, I'd moved the keys with them. Remarkably, that's indeed where they were the next morning - and not only that - they were lying there in exactly the same configuration as in my dream. A snapshot of the keys had been recorded in some neural pathway in my brain. Synapses had fired in my sleep and the image had floated into my dream. My unconscious mind had known where the keys were all along.

But enough of this amateurish parapsychology. If someone had told me that the solution to our quest concerning young George's death and the disposal of his body lay in our house at Mellor Brook, I'd have dismissed him as a fruitcake. But that is what happened.

The morning after my last meeting with Will, I took his advice and went down to Blackburn Public Libraries. That place should get a medal. Not only had it been invaluable in helping me develop my reading as a child, it had been a venerable institution since Victorian Times, feeding the passion for self-improvement that had seen many a worker attending evening classes, despite punishing hours of labour, and catching up on their reading and research in the sanctum of the reading room.

With the help of a Library assistant, I found what I was looking for. She told me that there was a printed list which is a copy of the Book of Remembrance kept on display in the entrance to the old Town Hall. However, this does not record the dates of the servicemen's deaths. A more detailed resource is a collection of cuttings from local newspapers, diligently compiled by the Library staff. Most of the cards include a photograph, together with the name of the soldier, details of his family, where known, and, crucially, the date of death. I was allowed to look through this card index and found it a humbling experience.

It did not take me long to find the entry for my great grandfather. There was a photograph of Corporal Daniel Catlow, who had served with the 11th East Lancashires, and who had indeed perished on the first day of the Battle of the Somme. It was a studio portrait of a handsome man in his early thirties, presumably taken when he had joined up in 1914. A note said that he left a wife, Maisie, and two children, Thomas and Cassandra.

The bizarre thing is that I could have sworn that I had seen that selfsame photograph somewhere before, but how and where? I must say that it rather spooked me.

Back home, Ruth showed an interest that she hadn't done before. Up till now she had taken a slightly patronising view, calling me and Will 'Morse and Lewis', and declaring that at least our 'little game' stopped us getting into mischief. She is an excellent woman and I am a lucky man but she does sometimes take a lofty and disparaging view of the male of the species.

I think her interest had been aroused by the family tree. After all, these people were her children's ancestors too. As she sat with me over coffee at the dining room table, she suddenly said: 'Why don't you have a look at Auntie Cassie's boxes?'

'But they were full of junk,' I said.

'We thought so at the time but we didn't know what we know now,' she said. 'You never know, Tom. You might find some leads in there. I'm sure there was a photograph album.'

'Yeah, but didn't we decide we didn't know a single person in there? Church parades and knitting circles and what have you.'

'Go and get them.'

'But...'

'Don't be stubborn, Tom.'

When my wife issues a command, there is no point in arguing. However, that didn't prevent me from making plaintive protests as I dug out the stepladder and went up into the loft.

'Oh, stop moaning,' Ruth said. 'You're like an old woman.'

I was going to point out that such a statement rather damaged her feminist credentials but thought better of it. It would only lead to a lecture.

The roof space is big and there is a lot of clutter up there. I had no idea where the boxes were and had to grope about for a while before I found them covered in dust, behind an old bicycle of Lisa's and a crate of books belonging to Nicholas which he said he must collect one day but never did.

I pulled the boxes out and manhandled them down to Ruth who was halfway up the ladder. There was a comical moment when a cluster of spiders fell into her hair along with a cloud of dust. Well, I found it funny. Ruth had a dramatic sense of humour failure.

Great Aunt Cassandra's legacy had long been a bit of a joke itself. She had left three boxes of stuff to my father when she died in 1990 and when my parents passed on they came to us. Mum had always said that it was just lumber but that she hadn't the heart to take it all to a charity shop and so it came to us.

We had looked through it at the time and decided Mum was right. It had been five years since it had seen the light of day. When Ruth had brushed dust and arachnids out of her hair, we heaved the boxes onto the table and began to rummage.

On top of the biggest box was her sewing basket. There was a scrapbook of knitting patterns and another of recipes, along with several packets of dressmaking patterns. There was a set of old-fashioned kitchen scales with their weights still in the original box. There was a little mauve reticule that I found impossible to associate with my great aunt, and many sombre headscarves wrapped in tissue paper. There was a dog-eared copy of Charles Kingsley's mawkish *The Water Babies* and programmes for various concerts at King George's Hall, which I thought the Library might like. But, on the whole, I couldn't see for the life of me why Cassandra thought anyone might want this flotsam and jetsam.

And then Ruth let out a little cry.

'Oh look, Tom! Look at this!'

In another box she had found a toffee tin containing a cheap necklace of glass beads, an empty locket, and a pair of clip-on earrings in the shape of shells. There was also a brown envelope from which Ruth had pulled a military cap badge. It featured a sphinx with the word Egypt underneath and a Lancashire rose below that. Underneath a wreath of bay leaves were the words: 'East Lancashire' and on top was a crown. The badge was badly tarnished.

'Daniel's surely?' I said.

Ruth nodded. I could see that her eyes were filling up.

Underneath the tin in Ruth's box was the remembered photo album.

She lifted it out carefully and we turned the pages until, leaping out at me now, there was the very photograph of Daniel that I had seen in the newspaper clipping that morning. Only, this was the original, still glossy if a little yellowed. I saw that one of the hinges had come loose and I lifted it, thinking to glue it back in place, when I saw that there was something behind it.

It was a letter. It comprised several pages of very thin paper, torn and very dirty. It had the official stamp to show that it had been read by a junior officer although there were no redactions. I unfolded it with the greatest of care.

1916   LETTER

My own dear sweet Maisie,

Sometimes your darling letters take what seems forever to get to me and sometimes I get two or three at once and until they arrive I think you must have forgotten me and found another man! I am only joking sweetheart because I know you are true as I am to you but this separation is hellish and it has been so long since my last leave that my heart aches for you something chronic. I hope my letters get to you without too much delay. I write to you as often as I can.

This morning it is hard to concentrate but I started this letter at first light and will keep on until I have to stop. Thank you for the parcel you sent me. You are so thoughtful, my love, and I think you must have made some sacrifices to put it together. It arrived safely and was not bashed about as sometimes happens. I was grateful for the cocoa and the potted meat and the fags, of course. The cake you made with your own dear hands was angel's food. I shared it with my mates in the section and they said it was delicious and they all want to marry you but I said they couldn't have you, Maisie, because you are mine alone. Most of all I want to say thank you for the lice powder. It seems to have done the trick, which is champion because you have no idea how maddening the little bleeders can be.

I hope this finds you well and feeling brave, dear one, because I need to tell you some things which will not be comfortable. You will soon see why. For three days, the heavy artillery have been bombarding Jerry like billy-o. They mean to soften him up by blowing his trenches to smithereens. Last night we came down the line to the front and in a couple of hours we are going over the top. The officers say it will be a piece of cake but I am not so sure.

Thing is I have a terrible feeling I might not make it. It's not that I am all that afraid for myself - though you'd be an idiot not to have the jitters with all this racket going on. I mean to do my duty like any man. What I'm afraid of is that I might never see your sweet face again, nor the faces of our Cassie and little Thomas. That is what is so hard to take and I cannot bear the thought of my little family having no-one to protect them.

I promise that if I come through I will find a way to send you a telegram which will get to you before this letter and so put your mind at rest. I don't want you to fret if there's no need.

My darling, I have something to tell you which I need to get off my chest in case the worst happens. It is something that happened when we were kids and which I have kept from everybody ever since. One day, me and my friends were on the canal towpath at the bottom of Bennington Street. There were five of us, me, Rob, Richard, James and little George - no, not

Rob. He'd gone home. It wouldn't have happened if Rob had been there. Him and George were thick as thieves. You'd have laughed if you'd have seen them together. Rob was the tallest of us by a long way and George didn't even come up to his shoulder.

Anyway there was this crane and I decided to give George a ride on this great hook. He thought it was for a laugh but I thought I was going to teach him a lesson. He was a terrible chatterbox you see and he was getting on my wick. God help me, I never meant what happened.

My dearest, this is hard to write. I am afraid that you will hate me for it but the fear that I might die this day is strong on me and there must needs be a clean slate. I cannot leave this world on a lie, my love. Especially a lie to you.

I have told the padre about all this and he says that there should be no secrets between a man and his wife. He has heard my confession formally and given me an absolution. He says he has the power to do this even though we are C of E. But he insisted I come clean with you and seek your forgiveness.

It's no excuse, I know, but all this happened soon after my dad was found hanged. I told you about that. Auntie Elsie did her best to look after me but what with that and Mum dying before, I was going crazy with grief. It felt so wrong that it turned me cruel. I pretended that the crane was a kind of ride and I got George to stand on the hook and winched him higher and higher. At first he loved it and then he got scared and started whining. I asked James to help me and I swung the crane out over the water. James already had a heartless streak and anyway, he wanted to get back into my good books. We had fallen out over something, I forget what.

I don't know what got into me but I told George we were going for our tea and James and I left him there and went into a tunnel up ahead. I deserve to rot in hell for that. I only meant to leave George dangling for a minute or so. Richard tried to swing him back to the bank but he wasn't strong enough on his own. He came running after us and threatened to beat me up if we didn't go straight back and help him get George onto the bank. He was almost crying with rage and made me realise what a horrible thing we'd done.

Oh, Christ forgive me, Lord Jesus Christ forgive me, and you sweet girl, forgive me, or my soul will perish.

When we got back to the crane it was clear that George had slipped, the hook had caught in his clothing and he was hanging upside down with his head in the water. We swung him onto the bank and tried to revive him but he was gone. We'd only left him for a few minutes. It was all a terrible accident. We'd meant to shut him up, not kill him.

What we did next was even worse. It has me shaking just thinking about it...

And damn and blast this bloody bombardment. It's turning my brain to slush and I must finish this letter. I wonder you can't hear it up there booming and banging around our beautiful hills and fells. Maisie, I miss you so.

George was as dead as dead can be. Me and James were going crazy. It was Richard who took charge. We couldn't confess to this, he said. The authorities would never believe that this was a game gone wrong. They'd call it murder. We'd be whipped and sent to a reformatory at best. More likely we'd be transported or even hanged.

Richard said we had to get Georgie well away from where we lived. James said we should just throw him in the canal. If he was found, people would just assume it was an accident, but Richard said it was too near our own doorstep. We had to get him away.

So we took turns to carry him on our shoulders, just like Rob used to carry him when he was tired. Of course he would be floppy but Richard said that if we were seen it would look as if he'd fallen asleep and that's why we were carrying him.

It was a quiet hour in any case. People were having their tea and it was too early yet for people to think about heading for the pubs. We stayed with the tow path until we got to River Street. This was the trickiest part. We would have to come out on the streets and down Cicely Lane to get across the main road at Eanam.

We needn't have worried. There were people about but nobody paid us the slightest attention. We crossed the tram lines and went all the way up Manner Sutton Street. Up there it was as quiet as a Sunday. I was carrying George by now and his legs were as cold as anything and I fancied he was getting heavier.

It was Richard who was making the decisions now, although I don't think he had any clear plan of action. We crossed Trinity Street and reached Larkhill. I think Richard was planning to cart George up to the tops where we could bury him and we could see the green fields from where we stood. But we were too exhausted to go any further. There was no chance we could get him across Penny Street, down Brookhouse and up Earl Street. It was really steep. Richard called for a rest. We turned into a back street.

Then Richard noticed that the door to a lavvy at the end had been left open. We went in there and Richard said this was as good as anything, better even, because no-one would go rooting about in a bog. We threw him in, Maisie, me and James. He sank out of sight almost immediately but we could still see one white hand.

There was a bucket of earth and ashes at the side with a rusty trowel sticking out of it. Richard shovelled earth into the bench-hole until the hand was covered. It was full of flies in there and it stank. We came away.

Richard said it would do no good to tell Rob what had happened. He loved little George to bits and he would go wild and maybe kill us all. We didn't speak again all the way home except to swear that we would never tell anyone what had happened. We would just say that we had left George by the canal and gone home by the road. I have not told a soul till now, my love.

Richard went to the Grammar School and we didn't see much of him after that. I believe he left Blackburn altogether in the end and we never heard from him again. He was not anything like as guilty as me and James.

There were times in the years that followed when I thought that the secret would make me run mad and you must believe me that if it were not for you and the children, I would have done. James did go crazy and they put him in the loony bin at Brockhall and later, when he was 21, they moved him to the County Asylum at Lancaster. He's still there for all I know.

It will soon be time for stand-to, my dearest, and then we will go over the top. If I make it, I will send the telegram, I promised. When the letter arrives, you must keep it safe. One day very soon we will read it together and you will tell me that you understand and that you forgive me, as I trust you will, for you are all kindness and goodness. Remember that we were only eleven or ten. We were hardly old enough to know what we are doing.

If it pleases God that I shall fall on the battlefield, at least I will have made my peace with you and there shall be no lies between us. You must pray for my soul until we meet again in heaven.

Tell Cassie that she must be brave and help you look after dear little Thomas.

I send you a shower of kisses, my darling.
I am

Your ever-loving.
Daniel
xxxxxxxxxx

2015   EPILOGUE

RUTH AND I SAT IN STUNNED SILENCE for a long time after reading this and tears ran down my wife's face. He was killed in the push towards the enemy lines, probably in the first few minutes, and never saw Maisie or the children again. Whether she hid the letter behind the photograph or whether Cassie did, we shall never know but, as Ruth said later, there was no way that Maisie would not have forgiven him. It had happened when my great-grandfather was a mere child and there was no intent in what was a tragic accident and yet it had cost him a lifetime of silent suffering, cut short only by a needless death.

Before I showed Will the letter, I decided to undertake a last mission. I learnt on the Internet that the County Asylum had been renamed Lancaster Moor Hospital in 1948 and finally closed in 2000. Yet another brick wall, I thought at first, but noticed in the footnotes that its admission records and other administrative details were in the keeping of the National Archive at Kew.

I took the train to London the same day we found the letter. I wanted to know what happened to James before I wrote up the case and handed the details to the police. It took me two days to find what I was looking for. After all, I had no idea whether he had died in the mental hospital or not, and, if he did, when.

Well, he did. There was a brief entry concerning James Bibby for May 15, 1905. It seems that, for a couple of minutes, he was left to bathe, when a group of patients who had been waiting their turn decided to help out the nursing staff. Unfortunately they used boiling water and James died from the scalding.

It was so absurd that I almost laughed out loud until I was seized by the full horror of it. Three of the five Victorian boys killed in futile and nightmarish circumstances while still young. I thought of Peter Shawcross's equally meaningless death. I would have to stay another night in London. I was too distressed to travel back.

***

Will and I are in the Alexandra on Duke's Brow. It is a fine summer's day and I phoned him to say that I'd solved the case and that it would be nice to get out of the town centre for a change while I gave him the details.

The Alex is a great pub. The inside is old-fashioned and the frosted windows are all etched with an ornate capital 'A'. But the great thing is that outside there is a bowling green. The place is full of memories too. It was our haunt as sixth formers when I was at the Grammar School almost opposite. I think the masters knew we went in there sometimes but they never bothered us.

We sat outside and I gave Will the letter and told him about James's fate. He sat in silence for a long time as Ruth and I had.

The Northern Elements

We are playing bowls now - proper crown green bowling - not the soppy flat green kind they play in the South. We are playing agains a couple whom I think of as elderly though they are probably no older than we are. She wears a skirt which comes halfway down her shins and a sunshade of green plastic. He has a golfer's diamond pattern jumper and cavalry twill trousers. He wears a knotted hanky on his head, whether ironically or not, I don't know. They are thrashing us.

From the East Lancs cricket ground over the wall comes the smack of bat against ball and ripples of polite applause.

I look at Will as he stoops to bowl towards the jack and I see again the little blond lad of years ago. What happened to George could have happened to Will. Was our gang so very different from the five boys from seven decades before? Only in peripheral ways, I thought. We are all made from the same elements. We all come from a fusion of gametes which have a billion to one chance of meeting. We pride ourselves on our free will but our end, like our beginning, is a matter of chance too. It's as simple as that.

My turn, and my bowl goes wide of the mark.

NOTES AND GLOSSARY OF DIALECT WORDS AND PHRASES

Wazzock A stupid or annoying person.

Moithering Nagging, bothering, worrying.

Double dog dare An intensifying of a double dare. Perhaps the 'dog' is there for its forceful alliterative effect.

Triple dog dare One step more binding than a 'double dog'.

Mar Spoil Now usually literary.

Sneck A latch on a door.

Mardy Grumpy, sulky, petulant.

Barm cakes and oven bottoms Flattish bread rolls.

Give over Stop it. You must be joking.

Red Indians Native Americans - the term is now considered insulting, though it would have been in common usage when Tom was a boy.

Skenning like a basket of whelks Whelks are large shellfish which in this context are thought to look like eyeballs. In a basket they would be facing in different directions so - 'cross-eyed'. Here: cross-eyed through drink.

Mizzle To rain lightly.

Dozy get Unintelligent fool - slow on the uptake.

Summat Something.

Larking Playing.

Bairn Small child.

He mun buck his ideas up He must buck his ideas up.

Childer Children.

Allus Always

Mumping about Moping about.

It's not going to put skid marks in our kecks [Vulgar] It's not going to frighten us. 'Kecks' are trousers or pants. The reader's imagination should supply the rest.

A pasting A beating.

Skriking Crying.

Wick with rats Alive with rats.

Do I 'eck as like want to give up I most certainly don't want to give up.

ACKNOWLEDGEMENTS

I AM, AS EVER, SO VERY GRATEFUL for the painstaking work of my wonderful editors, Julie Dexter and Peter Cheshire. If the slightest error remains, it will not be for want of scrupulous diligence on their part and if any flaw has managed to slip through it will be my fault entirely. As with previous books it has been a joy to work with such dedicated and professional people.

I should like to thank Mary Painter of the Blackburn with Darwen Library Service, not only for permission to use the cover image but for advice and encouragement.

I owe a great debt of gratitude to two closed internet sites: *Blackburn and District in the Past* and *1960's Blackburn - Where Are You Now?* The friendly and knowledgeable members of the sites have been an enormous help and their photographs and memories have been an invaluable stimulus in the making of the book. I have striven to be as accurate as possible with the history of the town, although in places, for various reasons, I have used fictional names and places. The characters, of course, are wholly fictional.

Magdalen, Norfolk
June 2019

The Northern Elements

Printed in Poland
by Amazon Fulfillment
Poland Sp. z o.o., Wrocław
16 October 2021

0c5ff529-64ea-4ead-8e6c-da08cefa8acaR01